Operation Firefly

While this fictional story is based on many actual events, certain characters, characterizations, incidents, locations and dialogue exchanges were fictionalized or invented for purposes of dramatization. Any similarity to the name or to the actual character or history of any person, living or dead, or actual incident is entirely for dramatic purposes and not intended to reflect on any actual character or history.

Second Printing

Cover Design by Larry Behunek

ISBN-10: 0996094903
ISBN-13: 978-0-9960949-0-0
ISBN: 978-09960949-1-7 (ebook)

Library of Congress Control Number: 2014937742
Foofaraw Publishing, Rhoadesville, VA

OPERATION FIREFLY

Liane Young

Foofaraw Publishing

Virginia

For:

Walter Morris—the first enlisted African-American accepted for airborne duty—and the sixteen men who, along with First Sergeant Morris, were the original US Army 555th Parachute Infantry Test Platoon, the Triple Nickles.

This is additionally for all of those who walked through the door they opened.

AIRBORNE ALL THE WAY!

PART 1: THE FU-GO

PROLOGUE

Honshu, Japan

April 27, 1945

Lieutenant Ito stared at the deflated, seventy-foot paper balloon anchored to the tarmac, and a wave of sadness washed over him. The balloon would be the last launch of the day and, if the rumors were true, it would also mark the end of the Japanese Fu-Go balloon program.

Before bombs were attached to the Fu-Go, thousands of Japanese schoolgirls worked in factories to construct the sixty-four paper sections, or gores, needed to make each of the more than ten thousand Fu-Gos that had been launched between November 1944 and April 1945.

Each girl meticulously laminated four layers of thin, long-fiber mulberry bush tissues together alternately lengthwise and breadthwise, with konnyaku—a potato flour paste to make a paper sheet. The dried sheets were inspected on a light table for imperfections—a thinly pasted area, a hair from the pasting brush. Anything that might cause the balloon to fail to complete its mission was marked and patched.

Once the raw paper passed inspection, the flawless square sheets were carried to the Kokugi-Ka Wrestling Hall or another of downtown Tokyo's large arenas, such as the Nichigeki Music Hall or the Toho Theater, where hundreds of civilian workers waited to cut them into precise shapes. Next they would seam together the six hundred pieces that formed each balloon and the encircling scalloped suspension skirt that held its shroud lines.

Every seam was checked and rechecked to make sure they wouldn't allow any gas leakage.

After the entire surface of the paper balloon was coated with a waterproof lacquer manufactured by the Nippon Paint Company, it was shipped to one of Japan's three coastal launch sites on Honshu—Otsu, Ichinomiya, or Nakoso—where a metal gondola ring, ballast, electronics, and bombs were attached to the Fu-Go.

Then it was ready for the launch pad.

As Ito watched his team ready the launch pad at Otsu, he recalled the thousands of launchings he'd supervised since he'd been assigned to the base five months ago, and he caught himself wondering what he and the other men would be doing tomorrow.

But that's something to think about later, he thought as he pushed the question from his mind. *I still have one more balloon to launch today.*

He checked his watch, noted the time on his clipboard, and then raised his right hand in a circling motion over his head. That was the signal the men had been waiting for.

A dozen soldiers quickly moved onto the launch pad and began repeating the tasks they had already performed twenty times that day: four men moved two 130-pound hydrogen gas cylinders from the edge of the tarmac to the launch pad; two men quickly removed the inflation tubing from the balloon and attached it to a manifold, high-pressure hose and a gas valve attached to the gas cylinders; four men checked the anchor and tether lines; and two men checked the gondola and the armament payload suspended from the rocker arm of a wooden stand on the edge of the launch pad.

As each group finished, its men bowed in Ito's direction, stepped off the launch pad, and awaited his next signal, which wouldn't come until he double-checked his clipboard.

When reassured everything was ready, he raised his arm and again made a small circling motion above his head.

One man stepped forward and turned the gas valve to the "on" position, and a moment later, the hose lying on the tarmac jumped to life as the gas coursed through on its way to the balloon.

The empty cylinders were quickly replaced two at a time from the stockpile of fifty-two full cylinders lying nearby.

Within minutes, the paper balloon awakened, gently unfolding and rising from its dormant position on the ground. As it filled, a large, black kanji character appeared on its expanding side.

Ito wrote the character on his clipboard and then looked at it for a long moment. *Wind. The omen for change,* he thought.

The balloon continued to ascend slowly off the tarmac until it swallowed the last gulps from the two cylinders lying on the ground. Rising from the eight thousand cubic feet of hydrogen gas inside its paper sphere, the balloon was finally able to lift the gondola off of the wooden rig and free itself from its earthly constraints as its shroud lines pulled taut. Thirty seconds later, the tether lines that anchored the gondola to the ground tightened. The upward movement of the balloon and gondola was stopped two feet above the tarmac.

Ito took a deep breath, walked forward, and began his slow walk around the Fu-Go, visually checking the lines, ring, gondola, and the payload.

Everything looks fine. He handed his clipboard to a nearby soldier. Now he needed to check everything again using his hands as well as his eyes. This time it was official.

Shroud lines—straight. Check

Gondola secured to aluminum ring. He touched the lines and knots. Check.

Thirty-six sand-filled ballast bags attached to the gondola. He caressed each bag, giving it a slight tug to make sure it was secure. Check.

Metal fuse box securely fastened inside the gondola; switch "off." Check.

One fifteen-kilogram anti-personnel bomb and two incendiary bombs. Check.

Everything is ready.

Ignoring the beads of sweat that had formed on his forehead, he reached into the gondola and put his hand on the switch at the top of the metal fuse box. He closed his eyes and silently offered a prayer and then delicately moved the switch from "off" to "activate."

Ito took his clipboard back from the soldier next to him and noted the time.

He turned to the balloon, bowed almost imperceptibly, and then walked out of the launch pad's circle.

Six soldiers stepped back into the circle, and then, in what looked like a perfectly choreographed routine, they simultaneously untied and released the tethers that anchored the Fu-Go to the tarmac.

Completely free of its earthly ties, the paper balloon with it gondola hanging below began to rise, dragging its tether lines across the tarmac as though they were slithering snakes.

Ito watched as the white Fu-Go silently rose higher and higher into the twilight's fiery red sky.

Within minutes, *Wind* joined a long line of balloons that stretched toward the horizon, each soaring higher in search of the prevailing winds that would deliver them and their explosive passengers across the Pacific Ocean to the west coast of North America.

LIANE YOUNG

Leonard Creek Park

Bly, Oregon

May 5, 1945

After more than an hour of listening to the continual drone of chatter, laughter, and bickering from the five young teenagers in the backseat of his station wagon, Reverend Archie Mitchell let out a deep breath and smiled when he saw a sign on the side of the road announcing their destination: *Leonard Creek Park—One Mile.*

Next time I'm planning a closer outing after church, he thought to himself as he reached over and patted his wife's hand. "Almost there. You doing OK, Elsie?"

She touched the melon-sized bump on her belly and smiled. "We're doing just fine," she reassured him. "But it sure will be nice to stand up again."

At the end of the mile, another sign marked one of the park's trailheads. Archie made a U-turn and pulled the 1942 Ford Woodie station wagon onto the shoulder near the sign.

He turned around and looked at the kids in the back-seat, who didn't appear to notice the car had stopped. "The park sign says that the creek is just down the hill. Looks like a good place for a picnic and fishing to me. What do you think?"

At thirteen years old, Eddie and Dick were the old-est in the Sunday school class and always took the lead. "It's perfect," they answered in unison. Both back doors opened and the boys jumped out, followed a moment later by Jay and Sherman. Within seconds, all four of the boys were outside running around and pushing each other.

Joan, the youngest of the group, slowly got out of the car, looked at the boys, and crossed her arms over her chest. The motherly look of disgust on her face let the boys know that she did not approve of their behavior.

They ignored her.

"Harrumph." She turned away and swept her hands across the wrinkles on the front of her Robin's egg blue dress. When she was satisfied, she walked to the front passenger window and leaned in. "Mrs. Mitchell, can we have our picnic now? I'm starving."

The boys on the other side of the car heard her request and let out a loud, collective groan.

"Reverend Mitchell," Sherman said, leaning in Archie's window, "we came here to go fishing. Can't we fish first?" His three cohorts joined him at the window and clamored in agreement.

Elsie looked over at her husband and laughed. "They've got us surrounded. What are we going to do?"

Archie shrugged and turned to the boys. "Let's eat first. The fish will wait, and I'm hungry too."

Sherman scrunched his face. He backed away from car and turned to his friends. "Aw, gee-whiz. I don't know why we always have to do what Joanie wants to do."

"Me either," Dick replied with disgust.

Eddie tugged Jay's shirt. "Who cares? The creek's at the bottom of the hill. Let's go explore. Com'on!"

Jay turned to Archie, "Is it OK if we go down there, Reverend?"

"Sure. Why don't you boys take the fishing gear with you," he answered. "Just don't go into the water until I get there."

Without another word, Eddie, Dick, Jay, and Sherman ran to the back of the Woodie, opened the door, grabbed all of the fishing lines and tackle box, and then quickly raced down the hill, disappearing from view.

Elsie looked out of the window at Joan. "Sweetie, why don't you see if you can find a nice flat, shady spot toward the creek for us to have our picnic?"

"OK, Mrs. Mitchell," Joan answered softly. "But will you come with me?"

Elsie opened the car door and slowly swiveled around until her feet touched the ground. "Let me help the reverend get our picnic things out of the car first. Then I'll be right there."

"Oh, OK." Disappointed, Joan turned and slowly walked toward the grassy hill the boys had disappeared over just moments before.

Archie leaned over and touched Elsie's hand, which was resting on the seat. "You go ahead. I'll bring the picnic basket and blankets after I find a better place to park the car."

"That sounds good." Elsie started to get out, but hesitated and looked back at her husband. "This was a wonderful idea, Archie. We really should do it more often."

"Maybe we should." He put his hand tenderly on her left shoulder and gently squeezed it. "And in a couple of months, Mrs. Mitchell, we won't need to borrow children for a picnic!"

"No, we sure won't!" Elsie laughed as she slid out of the car and closed the door.

Archie leaned toward the passenger window. "Now, don't let me see you running down that hill," he chided.

Elsie leaned back in the window and then asked mischievously, "But Reverend Mitchell, why can't I run down the hill like all of my friends?"

Archie smiled, shook his head, and said reflectively, "They sure have a lot of energy, don't they?"

"Yes, they sure do." Elsie added teasingly, "Maybe you kept them sitting in Sunday school too long, Reverend Mitchell."

"I'm trying to get them trained early so they won't squirm in church like their parents."

"Archie, you are so bad!"

"I know I am. Just look at you."

"OK, you win." Elsie stepped back from the door laughing. "Park the car and let's eat. I'm starving too."

"OK. I'm going back to the old logging road we passed and will be right back with the food."

Archie pushed in the clutch but stopped before he put the car in gear. He leaned back toward the passenger window and called, "Elsie, you be careful going down that hill."

"I'm always very careful these days…Now hurry back with the food!"

As Archie pulled the Woodie onto the road, he looked in his rearview mirror. Elsie was smiling at him and doing her "tootles" finger wave from the top of the hill. He shook his head and laughed to himself as he pulled away.

When Elsie turned around, Joan was standing in front of her with her arms crossed and an impatient look on her face. "Did you lose the boys, Joan?" she asked.

"Noooo, Mrs. Mitchell! I've been waiting for you." She took Elsie's hand and began to pull her downhill.

"I found the most beautiful place for our picnic. It's not on the creek, but..."

Almost stumbling, Elsie pulled back against Joan's tugging. "Not so fast, sweetie. No one is going to beat us there." Joan didn't let go of her hand but began walking slowly.

Halfway down the hill, Joan stopped and spread her arms to point out a small flat area filled with wild purple violets and yellow buttercups. She took a deep breath and recited one of her Sunday school verses: "They sat amid the sunlit flowers of God's earthly garden and gave thanks."

Elsie smiled broadly and pulled Joan closer to give her a hug. "Joan, you really are something. If I have a daughter, I hope she's just like you." She kept her arm on Joan's shoulder and looked around. "You have indeed found a spot that is absolutely heavenly."

Joan smiled proudly as she took Elsie's hand again.

"And Reverend Mitchell will be so happy to know that you still remember the poem you learned last..."

Elsie's words were cut short by Jay's voice yelling as he ran up the hill toward them. "Mrs. Mitchell, Mrs.

Mitchell, we found something—something really big!" He shouted, pointing toward the trees at the bottom of the hill. "It's down there! Come on Mrs. Mitchell!"

Elsie put her hand on her forehead to block the sun as she followed Jay's pointing finger downhill. Her eyes finally focused on something that looked like a big, white bed sheet caught in a tall pine tree. The other boys were under the tree, tugging on what appeared to be ropes hanging from the sheet.

"Come on!" Jay shouted, motioning for Elsie and Joan to follow. He turned around and headed back to join his friends.

Joan let go of Elsie's hand and ran after Jay. "Come on, Mrs. Mitchell!"

"I'm coming," Elsie answered, but Joan was already too far away to hear. "So this is what I have to look forward to...running...lots of running." She smiled as she slowly and carefully walked down the gently sloped, grassy hill.

Elsie stopped behind Joan and put her hands on Joan's shoulders. Together they watched Sherman and Dick pull on one of the dangling ropes while Jay and

Eddie tugged on another one; each pair looked like they were ringing a silent church bell.

When the ropes finally yielded to their efforts, the crumpled, sheet-like object slowly slid down the pine boughs, closer to the ground.

Everyone raced forward.

No one noticed the faded black kanji character that had exposed itself as the balloon unfolded higher in the tree—their attention was focused on a three-foot metal ring with a strange cylinder on it that had just slid out from underneath the sheet and was now hanging just a couple of feet off the ground.

Curious, Elsie and the five young teens walked in for a closer look.

At the top of the hill, Archie appeared carrying a picnic basket and two blankets, scanning the hillside looking for Elsie and the kids. His eyes finally settled on their figures at the bottom of the hill.

He froze as his mind tried to put together the scene he was looking at—a deflated balloon with a kanji character, Elsie and the kids around the balloon, a large ring with a cylinder-like bomb hanging down.

Suddenly he knew. He dropped the picnic basket and blankets and began running down the hill, yelling. "No! No. No, don't touch..."

His words were cut short by a loud boom and a fiery, percussive explosion that threw him to the ground. He tried to stand up, but his legs were weak and shaking. He got to his knees and slowly pushed himself up and then—half running and half stumbling—made his way down the hill through the dense smoke and patches of fire, until he tripped and fell. When he stood again, he realized he had tripped over a child's badly burned body. Horrified, he turned and, through the smoke, he faced a nightmare worse than any he could have imagined—the burned and blood-soaked bodies of his other four Sunday school kids. He ran from one body to next one—Jay, Eddie, Sherman, Dick, and Joan. Their skin was blackened. Their clothes were burned and smoldering.

They were all dead.

He suddenly caught a movement out of the corner of his eyes and turned. It was Elsie! She slowly lifted her hand from the ground and softly put it on her belly.

He rushed toward her. Then fell to his knees and scooped the woman who was his world up into his arms. She looked at him through glassy, blue eyes and smiled tenderly as her body went limp.

He clutched her dead body to his chest and screamed. Then put his head on hers and wept uncontrollably.

PERSONNEL—Fremont
Lakeview, Oregon

May 19, 1945

Armstrong, F.H.
District Ranger
Bly, Oregon

Dear Spike:

The tragedy caused by the explosion on your District on May 5 called for immediate and carefully decided action by you and your staff. You showed good judgment and a cool head by promptly and properly reporting the incident to this office, by going immediately to the scene of the accident to render first aid if possible, and by guarding all entrance roads to the area.

Lt. Col. Bisenius of the US Army was very complimentary of the manner in which the Forest Service handled this incident. He stated that this was the most prompt and effectively handled case they had experienced. This was remarkable, especially as the loss of six lives was involved.

I know that three of the boys killed were members of your 4-H group and others involved were close friends of yours. This made the part you had to play more difficult. We all appreciate what you have done, and I want to compliment you and Jack Smith, Herb Handley, and Harold Powell for outstanding service that will long be a credit to this organization and to the Forest Service.

Very Truly Yours,
L. K. Mays
Forest Supervisor

PART 2: THE PARATROOPERS

CHAPTER ONE

Southern Pines, North Carolina

May 19, 1945

Captain Tucker Freeman had hoped that he would be able to catch up on his sleep during the ten-hour train trip from Atlanta to Camp Mackall in Southern Pines, North Carolina.

He was wrong.

He had tossed and turned all night, trying to find a comfortable spot to rest on the "colored" train car. But he didn't. The old leather bench seats were hard, well worn, uncomfortable, and too small for him to stretch out his one hundred-and-seventy-five-pound, six-foot-one frame.

In the predawn light, he finally gave up trying. He sat up straight and looked out of the window. But it wasn't the passing landscape that caught his eye—it was the reflection of the twenty-six-year-old, broad-shouldered man in a paratrooper uniform staring back—his own reflection.

He'd inherited his long oval face, slender nose, and light mahogany skin from his mother, Emma. His light, caramel-colored eyes came from his grandmother and her Acadian ancestors. He studied the reflection more analytically and wondered what features came from the father he never knew, or even the grandfather whom he knew so well.

Nothing I can see from either of them.

From an early age, his mother had often told him that he was very handsome—just like his father. But that was it. She would never say anything else about the man who fathered him, or answer any of Tucker's questions, no matter how many times he'd ask when he was younger.

By the time Tucker was eight years old, he finally accepted the fact that Emma's unconditional love, and his grandfather's stern hand more than made up for the absence of a father and he quit asking about the man no one wanted to talk about.

His grandmother and grandfather, or the "Major" as Tucker had been told to call him, lived in a five-bedroom, brick row house two blocks from Howard University in Washington, DC. The house had been a wedding present in 1892 from the Major's parents, who were hoping for lots of grandchildren to fill the bedrooms and their lives. But Emma Mae was destined to be their only child, so the Major and his wife spent their time doting on and spoiling her. So much so that after her first year of college, when their unmarried daughter surprised them by announcing she was pregnant and was going to look for a place of her own, the Major and his wife quickly bought the row house next door. They weren't about to let Emma and their new grandson move too far away from *home.*

For the first five years of his life, Tucker was cared for and pampered by both of his grandparents while Emma attended classes at Howard University and worked part time in the school's law library.

When Mrs. Freeman unexpectedly died after a short bout with pneumonia, the Major stepped in as Tucker's full-time caregiver, a job he didn't relinquish even after Emma graduated from Howard.

Tucker idolized his grandfather and relished every moment they shared, even though the Major ran his grandson's life as if Tucker was an enlisted soldier under his command. His need to lead was inherently a part of his being.

Major Henry Freeman had enrolled in Howard University in 1891, and by 1892, he and a dozen like-minded patriotic friends organized a military company that drilled in the basement of Howard's Clark Hall three days a week. Freeman was the company commander for the next three years.

He graduated at the top of his class in 1895 with a bachelor of laws degree, but his deep, unexplainable sense of patriotism continued to exceed his passion for the law. Soon after graduation, he announced to his parents, his wife, and his new daughter that he was leaving for Fort Leavenworth, Kansas, where he would join the US Army as a Buffalo Soldier.

His family didn't like it, but they understood.

Four years later, he came back to DC and his family with a bullet lodged in his knee, discharge papers, and a Congressional Medal of Honor earned for his bravery fighting with Teddy Roosevelt and the Rough Riders at San Juan Hill in 1898.

The Major turned back to law, but he never stopped talking about his days as a Buffalo Soldier, or drilling the importance of patriotism into Tucker. Without any discussion, when Tucker was in high school the Major secured an appointment for him to go to the United States Military Academy at West Point.

Emma was furious when she learned what the Major had done. She had given up her own dream of becoming a nurse when her father insisted she take law classes to help with his practice, and now he had once again made a life-altering decision for someone else—her son.

The Major was diagnosed with terminal cancer when Tucker was a senior in high school, but before he died he made Tucker promise that he would put aside his plan of becoming a teacher until after he'd served his country in the US Army.

Tucker entered the Military Academy in the fall of 1937.

After four long, lonely years at West Point, Lieutenant Tucker Freeman graduated just as America was entering World War II.

His first assignment was to head the Negro recruiting office in Philadelphia, and to his surprise, he enjoyed talking to the eager, young Negro men.

Like his grandfather, the volunteers were driven by a sense of patriotism he'd never felt. They wanted to serve their country, even if it meant being a cook or driver or taking another service-related, menial job. Thanks to the long lines of enthusiastic young men, every month Tucker's office exceeded its recruitment goals. After three successful years in the Philadelphia office, Tucker expected to be part of the army's recruiting effort for the duration of World War II.

All of that changed when a colonel walked into the recruiting office one morning five weeks earlier and handed him a paper with new orders: he was to report to jump school at Fort Benning, Georgia, and after graduation, he would take command of the 555th Airborne, a test platoon of colored paratroopers that had graduated a month earlier and were awaiting his arrival at Camp Mackall, North Carolina.

Tucker caught the reflection of the coveted paratrooper wings on his jacket and shook his head and smiled. *What a strange turn of events, to go from being a recruiting officer in Philadelphia to becoming a company commander in North Carolina.*

"Woo-Woooo!"

The long, high pitch of the train whistle and the metal-on-metal squeal of the brakes brought Tucker back from his thoughts.

His eyes moved from his reflection and refocused on the scenery outside the window. The train was pulling into Southern Pines. His stop.

He folded his pant cuffs inside his dark leather paratroop boots, laced them, and stood up. He straightened his khaki tie, buttoned his uniform jacket, and put his cap on. A quick look at his reflection in the window confirmed he was ready. He grabbed the army-issued, soft canvas Valpak that folded in half; he used it to carry his extra uniform and other travelling items from the overhead rack. Then he headed for the door. The trip from Atlanta had been long and hot, but it was finally over.

Tucker set the Valpak on the platform, stretched the kinks out of his back and shoulders, and took a deep breath of the cool, crisp, pine-scented North Carolina morning air.

It's nice to stand on something that's not moving under my feet, he thought, as he watched the other passengers hurry out of the first train cars, heading for the station. He suddenly realized how much he was looking forward to settling in and having a normal routine again. It had been a hectic month.

When the platform cleared, he picked up his bag and headed toward the *Colored Waiting Room* sign to see if anyone was there to pick him up.

He was disappointed when he opened the door and the room was empty. *But the train was more than an hour early,* he thought consoling himself. He closed the door again and walked to the street in front of station, where he immediately saw what he needed—a taxi.

The short, lean, gray-haired man leaning against the black 1940 Plymouth four-door taxi looked up from his newspaper just as Tucker walked around the corner. He stared, open mouthed, at the uniformed man for a few seconds then pitched the paper into the open taxi window and stepped forward with his hand extended.

"Good morning, sir. Name's Jasper," he said smiling broadly. "If you're looking for a ride to Mackall, I'll get you there for ten cent."

Tucker shook Jasper's hand. "I'm Captain Freeman, and that's where I'm heading." He took two coins from his pocket and handed them to him.

"Let me put that bag in the trunk for you, sir." Jasper reached for the bag with his left hand as he opened the back door for Tucker with his right.

"Mind if I sit up front with you instead?"

Jasper nodded. "I'd be honored, sir."

Tucker slid onto the brown, cloth-covered front seat; rolled the passenger window down; and looked out at the bright-blue, cloudless morning sky. "It sure is a beautiful day in Southern Pines."

"Spring is always nice around here," Jasper said, as he got in the car and turned the key. The Plymouth purred to life. "But in a couple more weeks, it'll be so hot and humid, you won't be able to catch your breath. So you best enjoy it now." Jasper put his foot on the clutch and was reaching for the gearshift knob when he stopped midmotion.

"Captain, I got to tell you, I ain't never in all my years seen no colored officer here before. And is that a paratrooper uniform you're wearing?"

"Sure is." A broad smile lit up Tucker's face. "I'm here to join a platoon of colored paratroopers. And there's dozens more—enlisted and officers—some that graduated with me, and some that were just starting the school."

Jasper shook his head. "I've seen a lot of changes in my sixty years, some good, some bad, but a colored army officer weren't something I ever thought I'd see." He put the car in first gear and headed down Southern Pine's main street, smiling.

Highland Scottish farmers had settled Southern Pines in the early 1800s, and although farming proved difficult, the agreeable climate and an abundance of timber kept them there. The coming of the railroad in the 1880s allowed their valuable timber to be exported from the area, and perhaps more importantly, allowed the import of people to Southern Pines' newly built hotel resorts. By 1890, Main Street was bustling with two blocks of businesses. Built of brick and mortar, each downtown storefront had its own unique architectural style. Except for the addition of electricity and plumbing, most of the stores—Hinkle's Mercantile, Davis Hardware, Biggs Feed, the First National Bank, and Buford's Restaurant—were exactly the same, inside and out, as the day they opened for business. They'd been built to last, and they had.

"Looks like a nice town," Tucker said, looking at the buildings and watching the pedestrians as the taxi waited for the town's one traffic light to turn green.

"For a southern town, it ain't bad," Jasper replied. "Everyone gets along pretty well. For as long as I can remember, we ain't never had no problems, if you know what I mean."

Tucker nodded. He understood exactly what he meant. Life was never easy for Negros, but life in the

South—he'd learned from his short time at Fort Benning—was especially hard.

"How long you lived here, Jasper?"

"Sixty years. Born when the town was just starting and never been nowhere else," he answered proudly. "And, I've owned a taxi ever since I was seventeen."

Tucker furrowed his forehead and looked at Jasper. "Really? You knew what you wanted to do at seventeen, and did it?"

"Yes sir, I did," Jasper answered proudly. "My mama always said that if we don't take control of our destiny, someone else will—and we might not like their choice."

"Smart woman," he replied, thinking about his mother. She too had always encouraged him to follow his own dream no matter what other people, especially his grandfather, wanted. And although she never said anything after her initial tirade about his agreeing to go to West Point, Tucker knew that she was still disappointed he hadn't stood up to the Major. *But then again neither had she.*

Tucker's thoughts were interrupted by the sound of a plane flying overhead. He looked out the window and saw a C-47 army cargo plane climbing in an ever-widening circle higher and higher into the early-morning, blue, clear sky. He watched until it disappeared from sight and then said, “The base mustn’t be too far from town.”

“A couple of miles is all.”

A moment later, the sky in front of the taxi was filled with a dozen parachutes opening one after another and then gently floating toward the ground as white feathers floating on a gentle wind. “They must be doing practice jumps today,” Tucker said, keeping his eyes skyward.

Jasper slowed the car and lowered his head to get a better look out of the top of the windshield. “You think any of them is colored men?”

“All of them could be,” Tucker said keeping his eyes fixed on the horizon. “We all look the same from down here, don’t we?”

Jasper nodded as he sat up straight again. “Deed we do.” He looked at his watch. “This has been some day, and it ain’t even noon.” He glanced at the sky again and muttered to himself, “Isaiah sure ain’t gonna believe this.”

"Who's Isaiah?" Tucker asked.

"My grandson," Jasper answered proudly. "He'll graduate from high school next year and is suppose to talk to a recruiter about joining. He always said he was gonna be a jumper. I said it weren't possible." Jasper looked at Tucker, "But, who knows, maybe he can. Maybe it is possible."

"Times are changing, Jasper. It's possible. Tell him to get a good education. Go to college if he can before he joins the army. Education will open even more opportunities for him."

"Where'd you go to school?"

"West Point. My grandfather—the Major—got an appointment for me to attend." Tucker's face saddened as he remembered the Major telling him that he'd opened the door, and promised the academy education would be worth any hardship or prejudice he'd have to put up with.

It hadn't been, Tucker thought and let out a sigh.

"The Major?" Jasper asked.

"That's what everyone called him." Tucker chuckled and added, "Even his wife and daughter—my mother."

"Well, he sure must be mighty proud of you now."

"He passed away when I was in high school," Tucker said. He then added wistfully, "But he made sure I would get an appointment to West Point, which I did. And now, for better or worse, I'm in the army."

Jasper pulled the taxi to the side of the road and stopped by a large wooden sign painted with bold black letters: *Welcome to Camp Mackall—Home of the Army Airborne Command.* He turned the ignition switch off and got out.

"Didn't you want to join the army?" he asked as he got the Valpak out of the trunk.

"Not really. I always thought I'd like to be a history teacher at my old high school. But who knows, maybe after this war is over, I still will. Someday." Tucker looked at the sign and smiled, "I guess you could say I've taken a little side trip to Camp Mackall, North Carolina."

Jasper watched as a second group of parachutes began to open above them. "I can't wait to pick Isaiah up from school today. He really ain't gonna believe that some of them paratroopers he keeps watching may be coloreds!"

"The door's been opened." Tucker smiled as he used his grandfather's words. "He can be a jumper if he really wants to."

"Oh, indeed he does. He's always wanted to. But, like I said, I'm the one that never believed it was possible."

Tucker unbuttoned the side pocket of his Valpak and pulled out a small cardboard box. He opened it and handed Jasper a shield-shaped army airborne sleeve patch, thickly embroidered with an airplane, an open parachute, and three number fives. "My new company, the 555th Airborne. Please give it to Isaiah from me."

Jasper smiled as his fingers gently rubbed the patch's white parachute.

Tucker picked an army paratrooper pin out of the box. *Do I really want to encourage this?* he wondered as he held it tightly in his closed hand. *It's his grandson's dream,* he answered himself.

He held the pin out to Jasper. "And when he does become an Army paratrooper, I'd be proud if you'd use this to pin him at jump school graduation."

Jasper's eyes welled with tears as he took the pin. "Thank you, sir...from all of us." He stood up very straight and gave Tucker a mock salute. "It's been an honor to meet you. And I hope to see you in town again real soon. I'd love for Isaiah to be able to meet you, and to thank you in person."

"Tell you what, give me a few days to get settled in here, then I'll see if I can't arrange for Isaiah to come out, meet the other men in the platoon, and get a tour."

"That would sure be swell!"

"Good. I know where to find you."

"Deed so, deed so," Jasper said softly, still mulling it all over in his mind.

He got in the Plymouth, started the engine, and headed back toward town, waving to Tucker as he passed.

Tucker waved back and called, "Airborne all the way!"

He watched until the car disappear from sight and then picked up his bag and headed for the Camp Mackall's main gate.

CHAPTER TWO

The five-foot-square, whitewashed, wooden guardhouse sat in the middle of the entrance gate. There was a window on each wall of the small building, two of which made up the wooden Dutch doors. In rotating shifts of eight hours, armed military policemen manned the guardhouse twenty-four hours a day, seven days a week, to make sure that only authorized personnel got through the gate.

The twenty-year-old military policeman, or MP as was printed on his armband, was dumbfounded when he saw Tucker approaching the gate. He'd never seen a Negro officer in a US Army uniform. He opened the bottom of the Dutch door, walked outside, and stared open mouthed.

Tucker stopped directly in front of the MP and met the younger man's stare, eye to eye. He gave him a few moments to remember protocol. When it took too long, Tucker raised his eyebrows. He'd learned at Fort Benning that this small gesture usually brought enlisted men back to the moment and reminded them that they were supposed to salute an officer, even a colored one.

The corporal responded accordingly. He snapped to attention and saluted.

"Captain Tucker Freeman reporting for duty to Camp Mackall," Tucker said, saluting back. "Could you tell me where the men of the 555th Airborne are barracked?"

The MP leaned into the guardhouse to retrieve a clipboard from a small built-in shelf. He flipped through several papers then stopped and looked up, scrutinizing Tucker before he spoke.

"Welcome to Camp Mackall, sir. Our commanding officer, Major Clark, would like to meet you before you go to the barracks."

"Thank you, corporal," Tucker said, not showing his disappointment at this unexpected delay. He wanted to meet his men, but the CO came first. "Where's his office?"

The military policeman turned and pointed to a line of buildings inside the gate. "The two-story building on the other side of the parade ground. First floor."

They traded salutes again, and then Tucker turned and walked through the entrance gate into his new world.

The parade ground that separated the headquarters building from the main gate was the typical open, flat, well-manicured army field designed for practice marches, reviewing troops, and ceremonial parades. However, unlike West Point's nearly one-hundred-acre field, Tucker gauged that Camp Mackall's parade ground was only about ten acres.

At the far right end of the field, a football game caught Tucker's eye. He'd been the leading rusher for Dunbar Senior High School's Crimson Tide team in Washington, DC, for four years. Although he hadn't been allowed to play at the Military Academy, he still loved the game.

He watched the quarterback throw a long pass that hung in the air long enough for all of the players to jostle their way toward it. The receiver made a leaping catch and was immediately tackled.

Tucker decided to take the long way around the parade ground—the ongoing game was definitely worth a closer look. Just as he stepped off the curb to cross the street, a black, four-door Ford convertible with the top down pulled up to the curb beside him. A young, tall, colored sergeant wearing a paratrooper's uniform got out of the car and walked toward him.

"Captain Freeman?" He snapped to attention and saluted. "First Sergeant Walter Morris."

Tucker nodded and saluted back. He noticed that the sergeant was a couple of inches taller than he was, and a lot leaner. His brown, almond-shaped eyes and smooth, light-brown face came to life when he flashed perfect, white teeth and began to speak.

"Welcome to Camp Mackall, sir, temporary home of the 555th Airborne, Triple Nickles," Morris said proudly. He looked at his watch and added, "Your train must have been early. I was just on my way to the station to pick you up when I saw you standing here." Morris reached down to pick up the Valpak and put it in the backseat.

"An hour early," Tucker replied, "so I grabbed a taxi." He walked toward the passenger door, his eyes following a thin strip of chrome that ran from the curved fender to the hood. "Beautiful," he said.

"*Lucille*—our company car—1939 Ford Deluxe sedan," Morris said, as he got in the driver's side. "She'd been in an accident and was a mess when we bought her in Georgia, but the men fixed her up real nice in their spare time." Morris turned the key, and the engine came to life with a roar. "Speaking of Georgia, how'd you like jump school?"

"Didn't. I never thought that there was a reason to jump out of a perfectly good airplane," Tucker chuckled.

Morris looked shocked. "You didn't request to be a paratrooper?"

Tucker shook his head. "Orders from headquarters. My detailer said that the 555th needed a colored officer—and I would be him—after I graduated from jump school."

Morris sat in stunned silence, as he remembered the surreptitious route he and his men had taken to get into jump school.

As more and more of the civilian waiters, cook staff, and guards at the Fort Benning Parachute School were drafted and sent overseas, the school's students were assigned to fill those positions between classes. It wasn't long before the base commander realized that the added jobs were taking too much time away from their students' main mission—becoming paratroopers. To alleviate the problem, the commander brought in Negro service units from all the nearby bases, and within the month, the school's waiters, cooks, dishwashers, and guards were all colored men.

When Morris and his men came to Fort Benning, they were assigned as guards to police the school's training areas and hangars. But Morris wanted more—he wanted to instill self-esteem in his men, no matter what menial job they were assigned. So whenever the school's jumpers finished using the training course, he'd march his men out and practice the same maneuvers they'd just seen the trainee paratroopers finish.

One day, when the school's commanding officer was detoured and went by the training area, he stopped to watch Morris and the men simulate jumping out the mock-up planes. As soon as he got back to his office, he sent for the first sergeant he'd seen there.

Morris thought he was in for an ass chewing, but instead the CO told him that President Roosevelt and Brigadier General Benjamin Davis had visited the school recently and, not seeing any colored faces among the jumpers, said it was time to recruit a test platoon of Negro paratroopers. The CO wanted to know if Morris thought his men could become paratroopers.

His answer: *Yes, sir!*

For Morris, it was a dream come true—the first colored paratroopers in the US Army. His men would no longer be part of a service unit. They would be Airborne.

Morris smiled and shook his head as he remembered how proud he'd felt that day.

"I heard in Georgia that you're the one who fought to get your guard platoon into jump school. Why didn't you to go Officers' Candidate School and become the company commander?" Tucker asked.

"Most everyone at Benning expected us to fail," Morris answered. "The CO wasn't as color friendly as the general who commanded the paratrooper school. And it was the CO who decided not to put me in for OCS until I had my wings."

Tucker looked at the sergeant stripes on Morris's uniform. He furrowed his brow and wondered why he was wearing them instead of an officer's bars—if he'd made it through OCS.

Almost as if he'd read Tucker's thoughts, Morris turned to him and said, "I graduated from OCS. Just waiting on the paperwork. Which reminds me, we need to stop by the CO's office."

"I heard."

When their car passed the ongoing football skirmish, Tucker turned in the seat to get a better look at the ongoing skirmish. He was surprised when the men stopped playing and waved as the Ford drove by.

Morris waved back. "The rest of the Nickles," he said. "They're practicing for Saturday's game."

"Our men? Really? Who do they play?"

"Any Negro college that needs someone to play against," Morris answered. "This Saturday we're going to A&T in Greensboro. I don't think we're gonna win that one though."

Tucker turned his head again to watch the men as they resumed playing. "Are the Nickles any good?"

"Not really," Morris answered sincerely. "We lose most of our games, but it keeps us in shape and gives us something to do." With a hint of bitterness in his voice, he added, "The CO doesn't allow us to do much else on the base."

Tucker's attention was suddenly drawn to the sidewalk, where a tall young woman with cinnamon-colored skin was waiting to cross the street. Her white, sleeveless, calf-length summer dress accentuated her long, thin arms and legs.

"Whew-y," Tucker said breathlessly. "Do you know her?"

She raised a gloved hand and waved as their car passed. Morris smiled and nodded toward her.

"I do," Morris answered. "Matter of fact, I had breakfast with her this morning. That's Pearl—Pearl Morris, my wife."

"Sorry, Sergeant," he said.

Morris smiled. "You don't need to be sorry, Captain. I'm happy she's my wife."

At the end of the street, Morris turned left and followed the wide, tree-lined avenue across the back of the parade grounds to the only two-story, whitewashed, wooden building on the street—headquarters.

Morris pulled the car into a parking place directly behind the review stands, near the front door.

CHAPTER THREE

The young, blonde secretary's gaze was fixed so intently on the open steno pad next to her Smith Corona typewriter that she didn't notice Morris and Tucker had entered the office and were standing in front of her desk.

The men stood silently, watching as her eyes followed the lines on the steno notebook and her long, thin fingers tipped with a bright-red polish flew without supervision across the typewriter keys.

After several moments, Morris raised his hand to his mouth and cleared his throat loud enough to let her know they were there.

The noise startled her. "Oh, damn," she said softly as she looked down and saw that she'd hit the wrong key. She opened her desk drawer to look for an eraser.

"Captain Freeman and Sergeant Morris to see Major Clark," Morris told her. When she didn't respond, he added, "As requested."

The secretary found her eraser, moved the typewriter's carriage up, and nodded toward an open door behind her. "He's expecting you," she said and started erasing the typo on the last of the three carbon copies rolled on the carriage.

Tucker and Morris walked around her desk to the open door with *Major Robert Clark, Commanding Officer* stenciled in bold black letters on the glass top half of the open wooden door. Tucker knocked on the doorframe and came to attention. "Captain Tucker Freeman, reporting for duty, sir."

Tucker immediately was taken aback by Major Clark's office. It was spacious and elegant and did not have an army-issued look. The heavy, brown drapes that framed the room's three tall windows complemented the russet color in the large oriental carpet that covered the wooden floor. The color also complimented the two low-back, leather chairs positioned squarely in front of the CO's large oak desk.

Major Clark sat behind the desk with his fingers steepled, looking straight ahead at the doorway. "Oh, yes, Captain," he said as he pointed to one of the leather chairs in front of his desk, "have a seat." Clark looked at Morris but didn't invite him to have a seat. Instead he turned his attention to a neat stack of papers on the left side of his desk and shuffled through them until he found the one he was looking for. He pulled it from the stack and then turned his attention back to Tucker.

"I'd say 'welcome' to Camp Mackall, but 'good-bye' is probably more appropriate."

Tucker cocked his head slightly and studied Clark with a confused look. "I'm sorry, sir, I've just arrived."

Clark sat back in his chair and a small, smug smile formed on his thin lips. "So you did. But there's no need to unpack." He continued to smirk. "You and your colored platoon are leaving at the end of the week for Pendleton Field, Oregon." He sat forward and stretched out his arm to hand Tucker the sheet of paper he was holding. "Your company's orders."

Tucker took the paper and read it.

Morris stepped into the room from the doorway. "Excuse me, Major. I thought we were supposed to join the 82nd or 101st Airborne in Europe."

The hint of anger in Morris's voice brought Clark to his feet. "Well, Sergeant, the war is winding down, so you and your boys aren't needed there." Clark's words hung in the air, and his look dared Morris to make another uninvited comment. When none came, Clark tugged at the bottom of his khaki uniform jacket, and straightened to his full five-foot-seven height. He turned and slowly walked to the window behind his desk, where he used the index finger on his right hand to separate the pair of shear white curtain panels that hung between the drapes. "You know, Freeman," he said, looking at the parade grounds as he spoke, "if it weren't for Roosevelt, all of you Negros would still be in car pools or mess halls." He turned and looked at Morris, then added, "Or walking guard duty." He walked back to his desk and continued, "I don't know how you boys managed to get into paratrooper school. You sure must have someone looking out for you."

Tucker smiled. “Well, sir, since I graduated from West Point, it’s Uncle Sam who’s been looking out for me.” He had a trace of sarcasm in his voice. “He’s the one who thought I should go to jump school and come here, not me.”

Clark glared at him.

Tucker was satisfied. It was time to move on. He lifted the paper with the orders and asked, “Do you know what we’ll be doing at Pendleton Field…sir?”

“Just like your orders say,” Clark answered gruffly, “it’s classified. You’ll be briefed when you get there.” The smirk crossed his face again, and he added, “But I’m sure it will be a job befitting a West Point graduate.”

Tucker had played the game of innuendos with other officers enough times to know when to call it quits. He rose from the leather chair. “If that’s all, sir.”

“Almost.” Clark retrieved a piece of paper and a small box from his desk drawer and looked at Morris. “Sergeant, it looks like you made lieutenant. Sorry I won’t have time to do the pinning before you leave.” He held the paper and box out toward Morris. “The CO at Pendleton Field can have that privilege.”

Tucker leaned forward and took the two items from Clark's outstretched hand. "As company commander, I'm allowed to pin junior officers." He turned toward Morris, who was standing in the doorway with clenched teeth staring at Clark, and said, "It would be my honor."

Clark stood up again. "Captain, expect a final inspection tomorrow. Dismissed!"

Tucker and Morris saluted and left.

As they passed the secretary's desk, she held a sheet of paper out to Tucker. "You need to take this to the transportation office," she said and then swiveled her chair back to her typewriter and resumed her staccato typing. Tucker glanced at her for a moment and then looked at the paper, checking to see if it was one of the triplicate copies with the erasure. It was. He smiled and headed for the door.

Morris followed him into the hallway, seething. "Sir, the men expect to go to Europe. You need to talk to someone."

"We have our orders," Tucker answered and kept walking. "By the way, congratulations. It's going to be nice to have a fellow officer."

"But, Captain, the men are ready to fight. They want to go…they expect to go to Europe."

"We have our orders, Morris," Tucker said more firmly. "Let's stop by the Post Exchange to get a new shirt to put your bars on—Lieutenant."

"Sir, you went to West Point, surely you know someone…"

Tucker stopped suddenly and spun around, his face just inches from Morris's face. "Morris, the one thing I learned from my grandfather and from my time at West Point is that we *do not* question our orders…we carry them out…period. That's why they're called *orders*."

"The men have been training for combat for more than a year, watching all the white paratroopers…"

Tucker stiffened. "Enough. I am obligated to serve the army until the end of this war. In the meantime, as I have already told you, I do not question the army's orders…and you will not question me. Is that clear?"

"Very." Morris turned away and opened the door to exit the building.

CHAPTER FOUR

Sergeant Lou Boyle studied the five cards in his right hand for a long moment while he stroked his pencil thin mustache with his left hand. "Well, I say we don't need no uppity nigger from West Point here," he finally said, throwing his cards down on the table.

At thirty-two, Boyle was the oldest Triple Nickle, and at five-feet-six, he was the shortest. But his deep, booming voice gave him an authority that made the other fifteen men, no matter where in the eighty-foot-long barracks they were, stop what they were doing and listen. "He probably thinks he's better than us and is gonna take over."

Corporal Howard Sawyer looked up from his cards and furrowed his brow. "Didn't they send him here to take over, Sarge?"

Boyle fished a new pack of cigarettes out of his shirt pocket, opened the pack, and looked around, ignoring the question.

Sawyer rearranged the five cards in his hand and stared at the new sequence while he rubbed his short, carrot-colored hair with his free hand.

The two other men at the table looked at each other and smiled. They knew Sawyer's tic. He always rubbed his head when he was dealt a bad hand.

Trying to act confident, Sawyer tossed a penny in the center of the table. "I'll open for one."

"I'm out," Boyle said as he put a cigarette in his mouth, lit it, and inhaled deeply. When he exhaled, the smoke curled above his head and found its way into the slender face of the tall, thin man standing behind him—Corporal Alvin "Dixie" Flynn—who was polishing his tenor saxophone with a square piece of cotton cut from an old T-shirt.

He scrunched up his face. "Jesus, Sarge," Dixie protested, waving the white rag in an attempt to clear the smoke.

Boyle disregarded the complaint and continued smoking. "Sparky heard some white officers talking—they said that more colored men are volunteering to jump school, but our new captain didn't request it—he was ordered to go there." He exhaled another puff of smoke. Dixie grimaced and moved away as Boyle continued. "Yep, he had himself some nice, cushy desk job and they kicked his ass to Benning."

"I heard that too," Sawyer added. He looked at his cards again, slowly rubbed his head and picked up the deck to deal more cards.

Boyle stood up and stretched, holding his cigarette in the left corner of his mouth. "They should've made Sergeant Morris our company commander."

"Yeah," Dixie agreed, fingering the keys on the sax, "he's been bossing us for more than a year anyway."

The rest of the men in the barracks muttered in agreement. Sergeant Morris had been tough. But they knew if he hadn't made them run the drill course at Fort Benning every day they may not have become paratroopers.

"Maybe we just need to give the new captain a chance," Private Martin "Willie" Williams said, feeding bits of a cracker to the gray homing pigeon sitting beside him on the footlocker in front of his bed.

When Willie volunteered to be the platoon's communications man on the first day of jump school, the Army Signal Corps assigned a newly trained, eight-week-old homing pigeon named Angel to his care. Angel had been raised as part of the Pigeon Service Breeding and Training Program at Ft. Benning—one of four army programs begun in 1942 to breed homing pigeons for strength, homing instincts, and endurance. By the end of the formal program, Angel could fly more than two hundred miles to deliver a message placed in a tiny capsule fastened to one of her legs.

During the next phase of training, Willie and Angel parachuted together.

Willie wore a special flight shirt with a large webbed pocket on the shoulder, where Angel was tucked away until she needed to deliver a message or stretch her wings. And she knew the difference.

Every jump Willie and Angel made during the last phase of training was a little farther than the last one, to gradually increase Angel's endurance. Once her training was completed, Angel was expected to be able to fly four to six hundred miles, if needed.

Willie gently picked up the cooing pigeon and walked over to the card table. He circled and looked at everyone's hand, then walked back to the footlocker, sat down, and began stroking the feathers on Angel's back. "Well, I think it'll be nice to have a colored officer for a change," he said.

Sawyer reached up to rub his head, relooked at the cards he was holding, and then threw them on the table. "I'm out," he relented, turning to Willie. "But at least the white officers left us alone. A colored one won't, you can be sure of that."

Willie took Angel to the window next to his bed and set her in the roosting box that attached to an outdoor flight box. He closed the wire door and turned to the very large man who was quietly lying with his hands behind his head on top of his perfectly made bed. "Jimbo, what do you think?"

Private James "Jimbo" Brown raised his head and lifted himself up on his elbows. He looked at Willie and furrowed his brow, taking a couple of moments to mull over the question. "I don't know. I ain't had no feeling about this yet," he finally answered in a soft, gentle voice.

Willie nodded and walked back to the card table. "How about you, Roger? You always think you know everything. What do you think?"

"I ain't had no feeling 'bout it either." Corporal Julius Roger replied, trying to mimic Jimbo. He tossed his cards in the middle of the table. "I'm out."

"What'd you throw that hand in for?" Corporal Lonnie Jackson asked as he whacked the back of Roger's head with his open hand. Jackson and Roger were the only married men besides Morris in the platoon, and over the last two years, they'd become best friends, as had their wives, Billie and Lulu. "Terrance ain't got nothing," Jackson continued his admonishment. "I say he was bluffing. You could of won with two pairs."

Private Terrance Foster, the platoon cook, carefully put his winning cards face down on the table with the other discards. "But now you'll never know," he said smiling at Jackson. When he was finished shuffling the cards together, Terrance looked up at Boyle. "I agree with Willie. We need to give the new captain a chance." He leaned in and scooped up a handful of pennies on the table. Then stood up, moved his white cook's apron aside, and put the pennies in the left pocket of his khakis.

Boyle, his cigarette dangling from the corner of his mouth, moved next to Terrance and said, "Well, I'm betting he's an Uncle Tom nigger." He turned to the others to finish his thought: "And that's more dangerous than having some goddamn cracker again."

Terrance opened his mouth to say something but stopped. He'd learned a lot about the men's personalities since he dropped out of jump school and stayed on as the platoon cook. Most importantly, he learned never to take any of the men too seriously—especially Boyle. Boyle grew up in the poorest, roughest part of Harlem, where he was too white to have colored friends and too colored to pass for a white. Because he never fit in with anyone, he was always ready to fight everyone.

Terrance was two inches taller than Boyle and fifty pounds lighter, but that didn't matter. He looked Boyle square in the eyes, smiled, reached up, took the cigarette out of his mouth, put the butt out in the ashtray sitting on the corner of the card table, and said with a self-satisfied smirk, "You're getting ashes all over everything, Sarge." Then he picked up the rest of the pennies from the table and walked away, still smiling. Terrance was the only one who could get away with treating Boyle like that, and everyone knew it.

"What the hell are you staring at?" Boyle barked as he turned around and glared at Sawyer, Jackson, and Roger, who had been watching the exchange with amused looks on their faces.

Suddenly, Angel began clucking frantically, diverting everyone's attention from the card table to the window.

"What's wrong, Angel?" Willie asked, quietly opening the cage door. He reached in and took the excited, fussing pigeon out. "It's OK," he told her reassuringly as he stroked the feathers on her back. “Is all this smoke bothering you?” He fanned the air. Angel calmed down and cooed sweetly to Willie. He held her up to his face, kissed her beak, and began making cooing sounds back to her.

Dixie put his sax and cleaning rag down scoffing as he watched the pair. “I bet that bird would be good—with gravy,” he said to Terrance, shaking his head.

Everyone laughed, except Willie—he drew Angel closer. “Dixie Flynn, you think you’re so funny, but you ain’t. Not a bit!”

The other men kept chuckling, and suddenly Dixie realized he had an audience. He continued, “Everyone thought it was pretty funny when I took her out and put them chicken bones in her roosting box.” Everyone laughed louder, encouraging Dixie. “Hell, you screamed and fluttered like some little girl when you saw it.”

“That was not funny! You about gave me a heart attack.” Willie opened the small wire door, kissed Angel’s beak again, and put her back in the window roosting box.

Dixie wasn't ready to let it go. He raised his arm and looked around. "I say we vote. Who wants roasted pigeon for dinner?"

At five-feet-seven, Willie was six inches shorter than Dixie, but he never backed down. "Dixie Flynn, you need to..." Willie abruptly stopped midsentence and turned his head toward the front door. A moment later, everyone else also heard *Lucille* pull up in front of the barracks.

Boyle walked to the screen door and looked out. "Time to welcome Uncle Tom," Boyle murmured. The men put their cigarettes out, pushed the card table against the back wall, and lined up beside the footlockers in front of their beds just as the door opened.

"Atten-hut," Boyle barked. The men came to attention. They stood ramrod straight with arms at their sides as Tucker and Morris walked past two rooms at the front of the barracks designated for noncommissioned officers, or NCOs, to the squad room where the rest of the men bunked.

Tucker stopped and looked at the sixteen men lined up on both sides of the aisle. *My new platoon,* he thought then smiled. "At ease, gentlemen."

The men moved their feet apart and relaxed their posture.

The barracks was eighty feet long and twenty-nine feet wide. The squad room had nine beds on one side and ten on the other. Tucker slowly walked between the two rows of soldiers, looking from side to side at each man. He noticed that most of the men were fairly tall and trim. Only three men were under five-foot-eight, and in sharp contrast, standing next to one of the shortest men was a man who was physically larger than all the others—he was six-foot-three, tall, broad, and solid. As if to counter his bigger-than-life stature, he had a very gentle-looking, round, dark cherubic face. Tucker stopped in front of him. "What's your name, Private?"

"Private James Brown, sir. But everyone calls me Jimbo."

Tucker nodded then turned around to face the others. "As you probably have already guessed, I'm Captain

Tucker Freeman, your new company commander," he said, looking from side to side at the men lined up along the aisle. "We have a lot to discuss, but before I continue, I'd like to give you a few minutes to offer your congratulations to," he gestured toward Morris, "*Lieutenant* Walter Morris."

The men fell out of line and surrounded Morris. Roger and Jackson were closest and immediately shook hands with him and patted him on the back. When they stepped back, a wave of others came forward.

Tucker watched. The bonds of friendship the men had with Morris and each other were obvious, as was the pride they felt for Morris. Tucker realized that he hadn't known such camaraderie since his high school football days.

It'll be nice to be a part of something like this again, he thought as he watched them.

After a couple of minutes, Tucker grabbed a chair from the card table at the back of the room and set it down in the aisle way by the last beds.

"OK men," he said as he sat down, "make yourselves comfortable, and let's talk about our new orders."

The men settled on the footlockers and beds around him.

Morris remained at the front of the squad room, leaning against the wall with his arms folded across his chest.

"First, I want you to know how much I'm looking forward to getting to know all of you. As I told Lieutenant Morris earlier, you men set quite a standard at Fort Benning, and I can't tell you how happy I am to be joining the Triple Nickles. My grandfather was a Buffalo Soldier, and..."

Boyle stood up and interrupted with an anxious smile. "Excuse me sir, I'm Sergeant Lou Boyle. I know I speak for everyone," he said looking around. "We are all very excited about having a colored officer, but we are also itching to hear about our orders. Where are we going, sir?"

Tucker was taken back by the interruption but quickly decided not to spoil the mood. He'd give the sergeant a pass—this time.

Jackson stood up and asked, "Yeah, Captain, who are we hooking up with." He turned to Boyle. "Get your money out, Sarge," he said rubbing his thumb and fingers together, "I just know we're goin' with the 82nd, and I'm about to become one rich nigger!"

Roger lightly smacked Jackson's head. "Nope, we're joining the 101st, and I'm the one that's gonna be rich," he said tapping his chest with his thumb and preening.

Boyle took a step toward Tucker. "Captain, are we hitching up with the 82nd or 101st?"

Tucker scanned the anxious men around him. His eyes caught Morris standing against the wall looking back at him with a raised eyebrow. He took a deep breath and continued, "Neither. We're not going to Europe. We've been assigned…"

"Captain, did you say we're not going to Europe?" Boyle interrupted again. "We've been training for over a year to fight the Krauts."

Tucker, his patience stretched, glared at Boyle, "You heard me correctly, Sergeant, we're not going to Europe." Their eyes locked.

Terrance quickly stood up, put his arm on Boyle's shoulder, and quietly said, "Sit down, Sarge."

Boyle shrugged the arm off and sat down.

Dixie stepped forward. "Captain, I joined the army just to go to Europe and fight. "All of us did," he said as he swept his arm in the direction of the other men. "We're all ready to lay our life on the line to win this war."

"I know," Tucker said as held up the paper in his hand, "But, like them or not, we have our orders. And we're not going to Europe."

Dixie sat down and turned to Roger and Jackson mumbling. Soon all the men were chatting to each other, and the din of their grumbling began rising.

Jimbo stepped forward and looked at Tucker with his head down slightly. "Sir, I told my family and my friends that I was going overseas to fight for our country." Tucker closed his eyes and nodded, acknowledging the big man's pain and disappointment.

Sawyer stood up. His angry face flushed with a red orange so dark that it almost made the freckles across his nose and cheeks disappear. "I promised my daddy that we were gonna get that Hitler a good one for what he did to Jesse Owens at them Olympics." The other men raised their voices in agreement and the pockets of conversation grew louder.

"Enough!" Tucker yelled above the chatter.

The voices in the squad room went silent, but the men's faces and body language let him know that they were not happy.

"Listen up, men," he continued in a calm voice, "Lieutenant Morris told me how much you want to go to Europe and fight, but as Major Clark said, the war is winding down. Airborne doesn't need any more men in Europe, but they do need us somewhere else." He held up his fist that was grasping the tightly wadded orders.

Boyle stepped forward and crossed his arms across his large barrel chest. "So, Captain, where are we going?"

Tucker met his eyes and answered brusquely, "Pendleton Field, Oregon."

The rest of the men let out a loud, collective groan and began muttering to each other again.

"Are we still going to be jumping?" Roger asked.

"I don't know any of the details about our new assignment," Tucker replied. "Except that it's a classified mission. We'll be briefed when we get to Pendleton Field."

"There ain't no war going on in Oregon, Captain," Boyle said, barely restraining the anger in his voice. "Are we at least gonna be guards again?" He turned to the others before Tucker could answer. "Or maybe we'll get promoted to kitchen duty with Terrance."

Terrance frowned. "I don't think I'd like sharing my kitchen with any of y'all," he said looking around, "but especially you, Sarge!" The men chuckled and began drifting into small groups to talk about their new assignment.

Tucker folded the paper he'd been tightly holding and put it in the breast pocket of his uniform, then took a very deep breath. When he exhaled, he walked up to Boyle and stood close enough to make Boyle look up to him. "Sergeant," he said quietly and calmly, "you seem to have a hard time understanding what I was saying, so let me say it another way as slowly and clearly as possible for you." Tucker paused for a long moment before continuing. "We are going to Pendleton Field, Oregon where we will do whatever the army needs us to do—without question. As I seem to have to keep reminding everyone here—that's why they're called *orders*." He paused again still maintaining eye-to-eye contact with Boyle. "Do you understand what I just said, Sergeant?"

"Yes, sir," Boyle answered loudly and tersely.

Tucker eyed the rest of the men. They had suddenly become very still and quiet as they watched. "Then you're dismissed," Tucker said quietly.

Boyle stepped back, turned, and walked toward the rest of the men. "Didn't I tell you?" he muttered as he passed Roger, Jackson, and Dixie.

Morris overheard Boyle's comment and shook his head. Boyle always needed to have the last word.

"Lieutenant," Tucker's voice brought Morris back from his thoughts, "please tell the men the logistics plan we discussed for getting to Oregon."

"Yes, sir," Morris said as he nodded and walked to the back of the barracks where the men had gathered to grouse about their new assignment. After he quieted them all down, he quickly went over the logistics that he and the captain had worked out earlier to get their footlockers and company equipment to their new base. He assigned Boyle, Jackson, and Jimbo to leave in two days to drive Lucille to Oregon, and took up a collection for gas and motel money. When Morris announced that the rest of the men would be going with the captain and him on the five-day train trip out west, the din of moaning grew again as the men dispersed.

When Sawyer passed by, Morris put his hand on Sawyer's shoulder. "Think you could help Jackson, Roger, and me find three bus tickets for a reasonable price to get Billie, Lulu, and Pearl to Pendleton Field?"

"Sure," Sawyer said with a nod. He was the go-to man who could *find* anything. Within the last three months he'd talked a college football team into giving the Triple Nickles their old helmets, a local junk dealer into a new bumper for *Lucille*, and a local bar into giving them two free rounds of beer one night in exchange for Dixie playing his sax there.

"Thanks, Sawyer. I owe you."

"You don't owe me anything—yet. Let me see what I can do first," he replied with a smile.

Sawyer knew that cross-country bus tickets were expensive, but as Morris headed for the card table that had been set up again, he was already working on a plan for getting them.

Morris sat down on the only empty chair at the card table, and Roger silently offered him a cigarette. He took it, tapped it on the table, put it in his mouth, and lit it. Jackson dealt the cards.

No one said a word.

This certainly isn't going as well as I'd hoped, Tucker thought as he surveyed the room and the small groups of men huddled together. His eyes stopped on the short, thin man who was sitting alone on his footlocker feeding a pigeon a cracker. He walked toward him.

"Private, I assume your feathered friend will be joining us in Oregon."

"That goes without saying, sir." Willie stood up and extended his right hand and smiled. "Private Martin Williams, sir. But I've only ever been called Willie by everyone."

"OK, Willie it is." Tucker shook his hand.

"And this here is Angel," Willie said lifting the cooing gray pigeon in his left hand.

"Private, it's a pleasure to meet you...both."

Jimbo, who had been lying down on his bed, stood up and joined Willie. He extended his large hand to Tucker.

"Jimbo," Tucker said as he shook his hand, "it's a pleasure."

"You need something fixed, he's your man," Willie offered. "He's also a seer, so if you need to know the future, just ask Jimbo." He looked at Jimbo, then added with a smile, "He even gets it right sometimes."

Jimbo turned to Willie with a serious look on his face. "Willie, don't you be funin' me. I told you I had a feeling we wasn't going to Europe, didn't I?"

Tucker grimaced. He didn't want the conversation to turn back to Europe. "Well Jimbo, I hope you have a good feeling about the trip to Oregon."

Jimbo's serious face turned into a smile that lit up his whole face. "I know that *Lucille* will get us there, sir. I take care of her, and she takes care of us," he beamed proudly, his dark eyes sparkling with warmth.

Tucker patted Jimbo on the back, "I guess I know why Morris insisted that you needed to be one of the drivers then. Thank you."

Jimbo nodded.

Tucker turned when heard the first notes of one of his favorite jazz songs. He excused himself and walked toward the back wall of the barracks where Dixie had just begun to play, "Midnight Symphony" by Lester Young.

Young, a former Count Basie band member and a tenor sax star in his own right was known as the *President of Jazz* for his innovative and influential playing. When he was drafted into the army in 1944, unlike the white musicians who were drafted, Young didn't get to play his saxophone as part of an entertainment unit led by Glenn Miller or Artie Shaw—he was assigned to the regular army. He was just another soldier.

Dixie leaned against the wall with his eyes closed, letting the music flow out of his soul just like his grandfather Abel had taught him. For more than twenty years, Abel had played sax with the Harlem Blues Band just about every night of the week, and Dixie was at his side there from the time he was nine years old. Although his grandfather's sax was almost as big as he was at the time, Dixie would pick it up and practice playing the tunes he'd heard the band play night after night. It didn't take long before his grandfather and the other band members realized that Dixie had the musical gift. They began teaching him technique, but knew early on that they didn't have to teach him to play with feeling—he was a natural. It wasn't long before Dixie's sour notes turned sweet and his playing started coming from a place deep within his soul. His grandfather gave him the sax on his tenth birthday, and from that day on, he carried it everywhere he went and played it every day. By the time he was twelve, he could play anything he'd heard live or on the radio, as good as or better than the original.

Tucker was captivated by Dixie's rendition of his favorite song. He stood motionless until it was over and then walked to where Boyle was standing alone. "Sergeant, Major Clark said that there'd be an inspection tomorrow. Are we ready?"

Boyle looked up, offended. "Sarge…Lieutenant Morris expects more of us than any white officer ever has," he stated matter-of-factly, "so we always get through them without a problem." Boyle moved a little closer to Tucker. "And speaking of white officers," he said just above a whisper, "Major Clark handed you a line of shit about the war winding down. There's a white platoon leaving on Friday to join the 101st in Europe, and two white platoons leaving Monday to go with the 82nd."

The stunned look on Tucker's face made Boyle smile. He turned around and walked away. Satisfied that the last word was his.

Tucker leaned against the back wall. He suddenly felt overwhelmingly tired, exasperated, and alone. He glanced around the barracks at the men he was supposed to lead. He felt their animosity. *This sure isn't what I expected this day to be like.* He hadn't been accepted, and suddenly he feared that he might never be—a sentiment that seemed to be echoed by the soulful Charlie Parker song that Dixie had begun playing.

CHAPTER FIVE

The six-hour train trip from Southern Pines to Washington, DC, was the first leg of the two-day trip to Chicago and was broken up by a four-hour layover and a train change in Washington's French neoclassical Beaux Arts style Union Station.

Completed in 1907, the station was designed by Daniel H. Burnham, principal architect of the 1893 Chicago World's Fair. The Main Hall that sat in the center was an almost perfect 120-foot square topped by a ninety-six-foot high vaulted ceiling. Adjoining each side of the Main Hall were two smaller rooms—the East Hall and West Hall—where three million travelers dined and shopped every year. The station also housed the Service Men's Canteen, manned by volunteers, where countless soldiers could buy soup, sandwiches and drinks for five cents or less.

After they grabbed something from the canteen, fourteen Triple Nickles passed the layover time stretched out on the long wooden benches in the colored waiting area with their heads propped up on their duffel bags, sleeping or reading.

Tucker used the delay in DC to phone his mother and let her know he was heading out west.

Emma picked up on the second ring.

"How are you doing, Mom?"

"Tucker, what a wonderful surprise! I wasn't expecting a call. Dorothy and I have been waiting for a letter though."

"Sorry, I didn't have time to write. It's been a hectic week. Are you doing OK?"

"I'm keeping busy," she answered, "but I sure have missed seeing you every weekend. And I might add that so has Dorothy. We're both looking forward to the day this war is over and you come home. I pray every day that that'll happen real soon." She added, "Remember

Dorothy's graduation is this week. I don't imagine you'll be able to be here, but I hope you can find the time to give her a call."

"I won't be able to call this week. But please tell her that I called and I'm thinking about her, and I'll write real soon."

"I'll tell her. Are you all settled in North Carolina with your new platoon? I want to hear all about them."

"Well that's one of the reasons I can't call this week," Tucker said. "I'm at Union Station on my way to Pendleton Field, Oregon."

"Oregon? Why? You just got to Camp Mackall, didn't you? And isn't Oregon an odd place for infantry paratroopers to be assigned? You are still with the paratroopers, aren't you?"

"Those were a lot of questions in a single breath, Mom." Tucker laughed. "But the answer to all of them is 'yes.' The platoon got orders to go to Oregon as soon as I got to Mackall. And I can tell you honestly, the men would agree with your assessment of it being an odd place to be assigned. They are not happy. But orders are orders, and they don't have a choice any more than I did leaving recruiting."

"My, oh my, I'm feeling a little stupid. I've never even heard of Pendleton, Oregon. Is it near the coast? Is it a large army base?" She paused a moment. "And what will you be doing there?"

"It's actually located about midway along the Oregon-Washington border. The base is named Pendleton Field, and I don't know why we're going there or anything more about the base. We're supposed to find out the details of our mission is when we get there. But I do know it's classified."

"Hmmm. Sounds a little strange, but I never did understand much about how the army conducts its business," she lamented. Then she asked, "How are you doing with your new platoon?"

He reflected on the last week and then chose his words carefully. "They were already a pretty tight group before I got there last Monday. And there's a little resentment. They thought the sergeant who got them into jump school was going to be their company commander.

Then to top it off, I had to be the one to tell them they weren't going to Europe. That didn't help."

"In other words, you all didn't get off to a very good start," she replied. "Well, as the Major used to say, 'leadership isn't about being liked, it's about results.' Just do what you need to do until this war is over, then you can get out and come on home."

"I can hardly wait."

"By the way I talked to the dean about you taking classes at Howard to get your teaching certificate when you get back. He said you just need to come see him as soon as you're ready." Emma sighed. "A dream come true—you home and teaching high school just a couple of blocks away. Dean Thurman also mentioned that if you were interested, he'd like to talk to you about teaching at Howard. He thinks you'd be a real asset to the university faculty."

Tucker's attention was drawn from his mother's voice to a voice over the station's public address system announcing that the Capitol Limited for Chicago was boarding.

"Sorry, Mom, but my train's boarding, so I need to get going. Please give Dorothy my love and tell her to write me at Pendleton Field, OK? I love you."

"Love you too, son. Be safe."

Tucker hung up, picked up his bag, and headed for his train.

CHAPTER SIX

The Capitol Limited train from DC's Union Station to Chicago's Union Station took seventeen hours and followed the historic B&O line through Harpers Ferry then the Allegheny Mountains into Pittsburgh before heading across Ohio and Indiana for Chicago.

In Chicago, the men transferred to the Great Northern Railway line, which would carry them nearly two thousand miles across Wisconsin, Minnesota, North Dakota, Montana, Idaho, and eastern Washington State before pulling into Pendleton, Oregon.

The Great Northern had its humble beginnings in the 1870s, when James J. Hill began buying small, bankrupt railroad lines across the northern states then laying railroad tracks to connect them. To encourage settlements, Hill offered a $10 fare to the flood of Swedish and Norwegian immigrants arriving in New York if they would come west and settle along his route. Next he hired experts to help the new settlers build towns and turn the rugged vacant land into flourishing wheat fields and farmland, thus ensuring products for his trains to haul eastward. By the dawn of the twentieth century, Hill had put together an eight thousand mile rail system across the northern United States and into parts of Canada. What many people had once dubbed "Hill's Folly" became Hill's Fortune when he completed a direct line from Chicago to the Pacific Northwest. Hill, who had come to the United States from Canada to work for a steamboat company when he was eighteen, became known as the Empire Builder.

Before the men left Chicago to head west, the Great Northern Railway hooked up one of Pullman's new troop sleeper cars at the end of the regular passenger train.

In 1943, Pullman had received a contract from the Office of Defense Transportation to build 2,400 troop sleepers, intended for enlisted men, which would serve as a mobile barracks when overnight accommodations were required. One half of the sleeper car had fourteen traditional bench seats divided by an aisle. The other half of the car had thirty bunk beds—stacked three high—four sinks, and two toilets. While the top bunk was fixed, the first and second bunks in each stack could be reconfigured into a seat during the day.

Tucker sat on a bench seat looking out the window while Morris sat across the aisle reading. The rest of the men were asleep in the bunk beds at the other end of the car.

"Hard to believe it's May and there's still snow on the mountains," Tucker said, watching as the train passed a long range of snow-capped mountains. "What was it? Eighty-five degrees when we left Mackall?"

Morris put his magazine down and looked across the aisle out of Tucker's window. "I just hope there isn't any snow in Oregon."

"Weather should be warmer once we're out of the Rockies."

The passageway door next to Tucker opened just as the train's metal wheels made a loud metallic screeching noise and the train began to slow.

Terrance gave a shutter as he stuck his head through the open door. "Boy, doesn't that sound just scratch your nerves?" He stepped in and closed the door to block the grinding noise as he continued. "We're pulling into Post Falls, Idaho, for water, and all the white folks are about finished in the dining car, so I'm gonna start fixing us breakfast. Come on down in about twenty minutes."

Trains with troop sleeper cars attached usually also came with their own kitchen car, or rolling galley, but since one platoon didn't warrant the kitchen car, Terrance was told to use the regular dining car—after the whites had been fed.

"Will do," Tucker answered as Terrance turned to leave.

The train's breaks squealed loudly again, and the men on the other side of the car began to stir as the train continued to slow. By the time the train came to a complete stop, they were all standing in the aisle way, dressing and talking to each other.

Post Falls was typical of the many towns James J. Hill constructed for the immigrant workers a half century earlier. There were six white, wooden buildings lined up side by side along one side of the track, and one of them—Meyer's General Store—had tendrils of gray smoke rising from its chimney.

"Morris, would you get the men moving toward the dinner car? I'm gonna go over to the general store and get some cigarettes."

Morris unbuttoned his shirt pocket and took out his billfold. "Would you mind picking up some for all of us?" He asked as he held a dollar bill out to Tucker.

Tucker looked at him, disappointed that after a week Morris still didn't know him, and said flatly, "I was going to." He put on his cap, turned, and left the car ignoring Morris' outstretched hand and dollar.

Outside, the engineer stopped Tucker when he got to the front the train and told him to wait while they finished connecting the spout from the old wooden water tank to the train's tender. Tucker watched as two men released the spout from the tank and swung the free end to the fireman waiting on the tender. As soon as the spout was hooked up, the engineer motioned Tucker that he could go. Tucker walked under it to the front of the engine and across the track to the general store.

Tucker stepped up on the front porch, and as he grabbed the doorknob, he looked through the door's glass pane and froze. Four white men in overalls were sitting in wooden, straight-back chairs around a potbelly stove were staring back at him. He hesitated, took a deep breath, stood up a little straighter, removed his cap, and stepped across the threshold.

The storekeeper, who was standing behind the counter dusting cans on the shelves, turned when the door opened. He put the feather duster down and watched Tucker closely as he walked in.

Tucker nodded to the four men sitting around the stove, and walked to the counter.

"Two cartons of Pall Malls and a carton of Chesterfields, please," Tucker said softly as he put two one-dollar bills on the counter.

One of the white-haired men who'd been sitting by the stove and staring at Tucker took his glasses off and slowly stood up. "Well, I'll be goddamn," he said, turning to the old bearded man sitting next to him. "Would you look at what we got here."

A chill went down Tucker's spine. He'd heard those words once before—at the academy. He'd been studying for freshman finals in the library and had lost track of time. When the librarian began turning off lights, he knew he only had fifteen minutes to get to his dormitory to avoid trouble with the upperclassmen who would love to slap him with a curfew violation. He quickly gathered up his books and ran out of the library's front door, only to be met by a blockade of three upperclassmen that had been harassing him all year. The leader of the three stepped forward and said, "Well, would you look at what we got here." The leader's two friends moved closer, and the same chill had gone down Tucker's spine then. Fortunately, before the confrontation escaladed, the librarian opened the door, realized what was going on, and insisted on driving all four of the young men to their dorms—*so no one would be late,* he'd said.

Tucker glanced toward the door of the general store but knew that no one would be coming through it this time to defuse the situation. He turned to the storekeeper, "Sir, I don't want any trouble." He pushed the money he'd laid on the counter closer to him. "I'd just like to buy some cigarettes, and I'll be leaving."

"Trouble?" the white-haired man said as he walked up to Tucker. He reached out and patted him on the back and laughed, sweeping his arm in the direction of his three friends. "Not from us." He went back to join his friends at the stove, shaking his head and still chuckling.

The other three men continued to stare until the awkward silence was finally broken when the bald man asked, "You're one of them coloreds that the army's sending to Pendleton, right?"

Tucker's jaw dropped. He was stunned. He couldn't believe what the man just asked. "How do you know where we're going?"

The thin young man sitting next to the bald man held up his newspaper so the front page was facing Tucker and he tapped it. "Says right here that the army is sending a platoon of coloreds to defuse Jap bombs."

The old man with the beard shook his head and looked sadly down at the floor. "That was awful 'bout that preacher's wife and them kids getting blowed up." He lifted his head looked at Tucker and added, "And by a goddamn Japanese paper balloon."

The bald man jumped into the conversation, but Tucker didn't hear what he was saying. He stood frozen in time while his mind tried to sort through what he'd just heard. *Could these men really know about our classified assignment? No, that's not possible. Did something happen since we got on the train that we don't know about? No. I read the local newspapers whenever the train stopped. This just doesn't make sense,* he thought. Finally, he stopped trying to understand and began listening to the ongoing conversation again.

"It wasn't the balloon that exploded, it was an incendiary bomb," the bald man said, snapping his newspaper in half. "Says right here that they're all over the ground from California to Washington—hundreds...maybe thousands...of them."

The white-haired man that had first approached Tucker turned to him and asked, "How many are there?"

Tucker was dumbfounded. "I…I don't know." He walked toward the bald man. "May I look at that paper, sir?"

"Sure, here you go," he replied, handing him the newspaper.

Tucker unfolded the paper and stared at the two stories on the front page: "Japanese Balloon Kills Six Oregon Picnickers" and "Army Sends Negro Platoon to Oregon".

The old bearded man leaned over to pick his cane off of the floor. "How long have you boys been defusing bombs?"

Tucker looked up from the paper. "I'm a paratrooper…my whole platoon is Airborne…not bomb disposal." Tucker turned to the bald man. "May I buy this paper from you, sir?"

"Take it. I'm finished."

Using his cane and the arm of the chair to help him, the old, bearded man lifted himself out of the chair and slowly made his way to Tucker. "So, if you're not gonna defuse those bombs, what are you gonna do there, son?"

The old man waited for an answer. When Tucker didn't reply, the old man turned around and hobbled back toward his friends by the stove. "Looks to me like the army might not have told them about the bombs," he offered.

The bald man smacked his knee with his hand and began to laugh. "Yeah. I think the Tribune might just know more about what they're going to be doing than he does!"

Tucker felt his face flush. He folded the newspaper, turned to the bald man and thanked him for the paper then walked toward the door.

"Hey, soldier, don't forget your cigarettes," the storekeeper called, holding up the three cartons, "and your change!"

Tucker went back to the counter and picked up the cigarettes and change.

"Good luck, Captain," the storekeeper said sincerely. The other four men also voiced their same sentiments.

"Thank you, sir," Tucker said as he turned to leave. "Thank you all."

The outside air was cool and crisp, just what Tucker needed to clear his head. He walked to the side of the store and didn't stop until he was sure he was out of public view. Then he leaned against the building and opened the newspaper to read every word of the two headline stories.

CHAPTER SEVEN

Morris sat alone at one end of the dining car, watching the rest of the men talk and laugh at the other end of the car. When the men were first assigned to be guards at Fort Benning, they were a group of solitary, unsociable men who did what they had to do without a sense of pride or even respect for themselves.

Morris smiled when he remembered the profanity that was used at least once in every sentence they spoke. He kept telling them that they needed to stop talking like that if they ever wanted to gain the respect of those around them. When he wasn't able to make them stop their continual cursing by appealing to their sense of pride, he came up with another plan to cure them—every time they used certain cuss words, he made them carry the twenty-five-pound baseplate of a mortar around in a backpack for a week. It wasn't long before the most offensive words were no longer a part of their vocabulary—instead they had been replaced by the word *baseplate.* The men called it clean cursing, because they all still understood what was really being said. Morris was fine with the new word. More importantly, it didn't seem to bother or offend anyone else who heard it—military or civilian.

He'd worked hard to change their attitudes, and in time it gradually, almost imperceptibly, happened. He wondered if their new captain would ever be accepted into the cohesive circle that had formed months ago, or if he would always remain *the outsider,* just like the white officer's they'd had before.

The dining car door at the other end of the train slid open, and one of the train's regular cooks stuck his head through the doorway and told the men to find a seat. "Train's ready to pull out. As soon as we're rolling, Terrance will bring y'all some coffee. Then I'll be right after him with your breakfast." By the time the door closed behind the cook, the men had already divided into four groups sitting at two pairs of adjoining tables, still chatting.

Morris turned and looked over his left shoulder as the door next to him opened. Tucker walked in and sat down across the table from him. He laid the three cartons of cigarettes on the table near the window and then slid the newspaper across the table. "Looks like our secret mission made the Spokane Tribune," he said quietly.

Morris picked up the paper and read the headlines. "Well, I'll be." He opened the paper and read quietly for a few moments. "What?" He exclaimed as he lowered the paper to look at Tucker. "We're gonna be defusing incendiary bombs?"

Tucker looked around to see if the men had heard. They hadn't. He turned back to Morris and whispered, "Let's not panic until we know more than what the paper's saying."

"But it says the information is from army headquarters. Hell, they probably put out a press release. All I know is that we're not trained to do bomb disposal," he said, throwing the paper on the table. "There's a special army unit trained to do just that."

Tucker offered no comment.

Morris continued his tirade in an angry whisper. "And if the army could put it in the newspaper this week, why couldn't they have told us at Mackall last week? Or gotten a message to us at one of our stops this week?"

Tucker sat back and, without looking at Morris, answered almost under his breath, "I don't have an answer."

Morris stared at Tucker for several moments and finally asked, "When are you going to tell the men?"

"We'll be at Pendleton in a few hours. I'd like to wait until I can talk to the CO there and find out more about what's going on," Tucker answered.

Morris continued to look at him with annoyance. "That may be too late," Morris finally said as the passageway door opened at the other end of the dining car and Terrance came in carrying a stack of newspapers.

"You're in the paper," Terrance said, dropping a couple of newspapers on each of the tables. "Says here that you're gonna be defusing Japanese bombs."

"What?" Dixie grabbed the paper on his table. He read the headline and then the first couple of sentences before throwing the paper angrily on the table. "What the *baseplate*?"

Sawyer picked up the paper Dixie threw down and read the headlines. "Bomb defusers? Ain't that a new one. I just love the army," Sawyer said as he put the paper down and began rubbing he head. "Do you think they know," he asked, motioning with his head to the back of the car where Tucker and Morris were sitting.

Roger grabbed the paper Sawyer put down and began to read it with Willie and Angel leaning over his shoulder.

"I'll bet one of them does. Let's find out." Dixie stood up, picked up another paper, and headed toward the back of the car, where Tucker and Morris sat. Sawyer and several other men followed. When Dixie saw a copy of the newspaper on their table, he looked at Tucker, pointed angrily to the headlined, and asked, "When were you going to tell us?"

Tucker remained silent.

Dixie put both hands on the edge of the dining table and leaned down, looking eye to eye at Tucker. "I'm a paratrooper. I don't know nothing about defusing no bombs, and I don't want to know nothing about it either."

"Man, I swear the army is trying to kill us," Sawyer said, leaning down next to Dixie. "Sir." He looked at Tucker. "You gonna talk to someone and get our orders changed when we get to Pendleton?"

Tucker shook his head. "That's not how it's done. Our orders came from Army Headquarters. They won't get changed at Pendleton." Tucker saw the men's shoulders slump and felt their disappointment. "Besides the paper could have gotten the story wrong. As soon as we get to Pendleton Field, I'll find out what's going on," he promised.

The men shook their heads and turned away from the table, grumbling as they made their way back to the other end of the dining car.

Dixie leaned close to Sawyer as they sat down at their table with Willie and Roger. "Sarge warned us. He's gonna get us all killed...that's his orders."

Willie looked up from the newspaper. "Com'on, Dixie, you know there ain't no order to get us killed. You're starting to talk as stupid as Sarge."

Dixie opened his mouth to answer but then stopped when the door next to him slid open and Terrance walked in with two large pots coffee and began filling everyone's cup.

The discussion was over.

Willie moved his empty coffee cup closer to the edge of the table and pushed the folded paper out of the way. "It really was too bad about the preacher's wife and those kids."

Roger unfolded his napkin and put it in his lap. "That's what happens when you play with bombs, and why we shouldn't do it."

Terrance stopped at their table and poured steaming hot coffee in the four waiting cups. "Man, I gotta tell you that this is the first time I'm really happy I dropped out of jump school. The kitchen is much safer," he smiled and winked at Angel who was sitting on Willie's shoulder and then added, "for most of us."

CHAPTER EIGHT

Dressed in their paratrooper uniforms, caps, and boots, Boyle, Jimbo, and Jackson were standing under the Pendleton, Oregon, sign near the end of the train platform waiting for the rest of the platoon when they heard the train's whistle blow.

Boyle looked at his watch. "Right on time."

"I wonder if they know about this yet," Jackson asked, pulling the newspaper from his back pocket.

"Oh, I'm pretty sure that the captain knows all about it," Boyle answered smugly.

Jimbo and Jackson looked at each other and grimaced. After a week on the road with Boyle and his attitude, they'd both had enough of him and were looking forward to seeing the rest of the men and having a normal conversation.

The train's whistle blew again, and its brakes squealed as they fought to stop the iron horse, continuing their high-pitched, metal-on-metal squealing until they finally won the battle and the train came to a complete stop. The troop sleeper car—the last car on the train—stopped at the end of the platform where Boyle, Jackson, Jimbo, and a porter were waiting.

The gray-haired Negro porter pushed an old, flat, wooden luggage cart with four large metal wheels toward the train door and parked it. He set a step down in front of the door then slid it open allowing Roger, Sawyer, Willie, Dixie, Terrance, and the rest of the enlisted men to eagerly leave the train car that had been home for three days. Jackson and Jimbo moved to the luggage cart excitedly greeting everyone as they tossed their duffel bags on the luggage cart.

Willie put Angel's wooden cage on the ground so he could add his duffel bag to the pile when Jimbo came up beside him and took care of the bag for him. He put his large arm around Willie's shoulder and smiled. "You ain't going to believe the flight cage and roosting box we made Angel. And we built it right in the window next to your bunk."

Willie lifted the carrier box with Angel. "You hear that, sugar, your Uncle Jimbo already made you a home."

Angel cooed.

"Thanks, Jimbo," Willie said. "I know she's looking forward to being able to move around and fly again. Heck, I think we all are."

"Soon as we get all the luggage, I'll take you 'round front. I got us a bus waiting."

The porter came forward and made a brushing motion to Jimbo. "Just you go on and go. It would be my pleasure to help you all."

"Thank you, sir."

Boyle waited as the last two men, Morris and Tucker, stepped onto the platform and then walked forward.

"Welcome to Pendleton," Boyle said, holding the newspaper out to Tucker as he reached for Tucker's Valpak, "home of the 555th bomb disposal unit."

Tucker gripped the Valpak tighter, and gritted his teeth. "Thank you, Sergeant. I'll get it."

The porter walked forward and grabbed the officers' Valpaks and smiled. He added them to the baggage cart and began pushing it toward the station. Tucker took change from his pocket and handed it to the porter, who pushed his hand back. "It's my honor, sir."

Tucker smiled, nodded, and then turned back to Boyle.

"We saw the article in the paper this morning," Tucker continued. "What have you heard?"

"Just know what I read in the paper," Boyle replied as he turned and headed toward the station. Tucker and Morris followed. "But we were sure you'd..."

Morris stepped beside Boyle, interrupting him. "Did you have a good trip, Sergeant?"

Boyle's voice and demeanor changed instantly. "Yes siree, we did. *Lucille* got us here without a hitch. We got in three days ago," Boyle answered. Then he proudly added with a wink to Morris, "And I already got the lay of the land."

Boyle led Morris and Tucker to the front of the station where the other men were waiting next to a small white bus with *Ebenezer Baptist Church* painted in large, faded black letters on the side.

"The army offered us a troop carrier, with no shocks, of course," Boyle said, patting the side of the bus. "But Jimbo's already got an in with the local Baptist church. They loaned us their bus to pick y'all up."

Jimbo turned his head when he heard his name. "They need some electrical work, and we need transportation," he said, smiling at Morris and Tucker. He picked their Valpaks off the cart then turned to Boyle and added, "And you always gets more bees with honey than vinegar."

Tucker and Morris looked at each other and smiled.

Boyle straightened up and turned toward the rest of the men who were chatting by the bus door. "All right, get your asses on the bus, unless you're waiting on me to kick 'em."

"So much for honey," Morris mumbled to himself as everyone boarded.

Jimbo put the Valpaks down on the first bench seat in the bus. When everyone was seated, he eased his large frame into the seat behind the steering wheel, pulled the handle to close the bus door, and turned the ignition key. The engine started immediately, and Jimbo pulled away from the station toward Pendleton's bustling main street.

Pendleton, located on the Oregon Trail, was founded as a trading post in the mid-1800s along the Umatilla River. In 1868, it was named for George Pendleton, county commissioner and the 1864 democratic vice presidential candidate. The town's population was just two hundred people when the railroad tracks were laid in the 1870s. But by 1909, when English weaver Thomas L. Kay opened the Pendleton Woolen Mill, the town boasted over four thousand residents and included a Chinatown that had been settled by laid-off railroad workers when the rails were complete.

Tucker looked out of the bus's open window at the town's wide streets and the old brick storefronts. A smile crossed his face as he remembered that less than two weeks ago, he was riding down Main Street of Southern Pines talking to Jasper. He had been looking forward to a normal routine at his new base, and now here he was on the other side of the country with no idea of what his future held.

Jimbo slowed the bus when he neared the railroad tracks at the edge of town, and the men began to hoot and plead for Jimbo to stop at a one-story building with an inviting blinking red neon sign: *Twilight Bar—Open.*

"Forget it," Boyle said as he stood up and faced the men. "We ain't allowed to go there."

Jimbo stopped the bus and turned toward the men. "Pastor told me don't even think 'bout crossing them tracks after dark or you'll likely be looking down the barrel of a shotgun." Then Jimbo pointed ahead of the bus on the other side of the tracks and an old wooden, weatherworn building—Betty's Bar. "That's our bar," he said, putting the bus in gear again, "but she don't open up 'til five."

The men booed.

"Don't worry," Boyle consoled, "we'll be back."

Tucker tapped Boyle on his back. "What was that about the shotguns? Is it true?"

Boyle sat back down, "Oh, yeah. The town has what the coloreds here call—the '*Cowboy Guard*.' After dark, you'll see them standing by the tracks at the feed store. They protect the town…from us. They do the same thing around Chinatown. I heard that the Chinamen dug tunnels underneath the city just so they can get around after dark. Them cowboys see anything moving that ain't white or where it's supposed to be, they just shoot. No questions asked."

Tucker was stunned. "What? I thought that the West would be better than the South."

Boyle sighed. "Nope, this is worse. The town hates the Chinese who came here to work on the railroad, and that hating just rolled right onto us."

Boyle jumped up from his seat again and pointed at a spacious, three-story, Queen Anne–style brick house with a huge wraparound front porch. "That's Miss Rae's Rooming House," he said excitedly. "Lulu, Billie, and Pearl got here yesterday." He turned to Morris. "And we made sure they got real nice rooms there."

"Thanks for taking care of them," Morris said as he craned his neck to see if he could see his wife in the yard or on the porch. He didn't.

"Don't worry," Jimbo said, smiling in the rear-view mirror, "either *Lucille* or I will get you down here later."

"Thanks. That'd be great," Morris said with a smile.

Although the army airbase was only two miles from downtown Pendleton, as the crow flies, it was a seven-mile drive from the valley floor to the top of the plateau, where the base had been built in 1941 on the Pendleton Municipal Airport site.

During the fifteen-minute trip, Tucker kept an eye on the sky and was surprised he hadn't seen any airplanes flying overhead. "Who's stationed at the base?" he asked Boyle.

"It's bare bones. Only a few people, and fewer planes," Boyle answered. Then he added sarcastically, "But then, the war is winding down."

Tucker took a deep breath and exhaled slowly. It had been less than half an hour, yet he was already doing that a lot around Boyle.

At the top of the plateau, Jimbo drove through the unguarded main gate of Pendleton Field and turned right on Perimeter Road. The bus passed two blocks of empty, but freshly whitewashed, one-story wooden buildings.

Jimbo pulled over to the curb in the middle of the third block and stopped the bus in front of an immaculately taken care of building with a beautifully manicured lawn. A sidewalk edging a bed of blooming pink, red, and white azaleas led to the buildings double entrance door.

Boyle picked up the two Valpaks behind Jimbo, then turned to Tucker and Morris. "Bachelor Officers' Quarters. This is your stop."

"Sergeant," Tucker asked, "are you sure we're supposed to stay here?"

"Yes, sir," Boyle answered, "the housing officer assigned us to a barracks, but said that the officers was to stay in the BOQ."

The rest of the men moved to the right side of the bus to get a better look.

Roger whistled. "Now that's nice." He turned to Jackson and asked, "Does our place look like that?"

Jackson smacked Roger's head and laughed, "Hell no. We're lucky we got inside plumbing."

"You better be kidding, Jackson," Roger said, rubbing his head.

Tucker and Morris took their bags from Boyle and stepped off the bus, still dumbfounded and wondering why they would have been housed in a BOQ.

"Want us to pick you up for dinner," Boyle asked from an open window, "or will you be dining with your fellow officers?"

Morris looked from Tucker to Jimbo, "Pick us up in an hour."

Jimbo nodded, closed the bus door then continued heading south down Perimeter Road, passing more empty buildings and hangars. He turned right onto a crumbling road at the Company Street R sign then carefully maneuvered the bus slowly around the large potholes that dotted the road. He pulled the bus over to the curb in front of three adjacent buildings that had freshly mowed grass—a stark contrast to the vacant neighboring buildings that were overrun with tall weeds.

Boyle stood up. "Home sweet home," he announced in the sardonic tone that was becoming his normal voice.

As the men grabbed their duffel bags and filed off the bus to make their way to the barracks, Boyle stopped Terrance and pointed to the middle building. "That's our mess hall. We've been working with the service unit guys in the barracks on the other side of it to get it all fixed up again so both of us can use it."

Terrance looked at him curiously. "Where they been eating?"

"Oh, they been eating in there, but the cooks in their outfit work in the white officers' dining hall and enlisted mess, so they just brought the leftovers here each morning and night," Boyle said.

Terrance shook his head in disgust.

Boyle continued. "So if you'll be the main cook, all the service unit men have agreed to help peel potatoes and do any other KP duties you need. And the other cooks will help you every day, as soon as they finish their other cooking."

Terrance shrugged his shoulders. “That’s fine. Cook for twenty, cook for forty, it’s all the same. And I imagine they’ll have extra food to bring back here.”

“Yup. That’s why they never set up their own mess hall. But I told them that you’d never put up with eating somebody’s cold leftovers every day,” Boyle said proudly, “so I got Jimbo to rehook up the stove and sink, and we’ve put together pots and pans and dishes. That should get you started. And now that Sawyer’s here,” Boyle winked at Terrance, “he should be able to find you whatever else you need.”

“Let me take a look, but it sounds like I have everything I need.”

“Great,” Boyle said as he reached for Terrance’s duffel bag. “How about I take your bag to the barracks while you look the kitchen over. Then make me a list of whatever else you think you need.”

“Sure. Just let me get a couple of things out first,” Terrance said, unzipping the bag. He pulled his white cook’s apron and baker’s hat out, zipped the bag then headed toward the middle building, as he called over his shoulder, "If everything's here like you said, then I should have dinner ready by 1700."

There were four standard floor plans for Mobilization Buildings, or mess halls, which were designed for seating 118, 170, 210, or 250 men on wooden mess tables with built-in benches. When Terrance walked in the building, he immediately knew that their mess hall was the smaller 118-man floor plan, which was still more than twice what was needed for the Triple Nickles and the service unit combined.

Like all army buildings built between 1940 and 1945, the seventy-four-foot by twenty-five-foot, one-story wood mess hall was built—from its concrete slab to its shingled roof—to the exact specifications directed by the army's Mobilization Buildings plan.

Terrance walked through the front door into the bright, sun-lit dining area and then down the center aisle created by the pairs of tables on each side of the room until he came to the waist-high metal service counter and service window that separated the kitchen from the dining room. He put his hands on the counter and looked through the window at the kitchen. All of the appliances were in place, pots and pans were hanging neatly on a rack over the cook's table, the cutlery and other utensils were laid out on a butcher block, and dishes were stacked by the service counter window. Boyle and the men had done a good job. Terrance smiled as he put his apron and hat on.

"Now let's see what we can find to cook in this fine kitchen," he said to himself as he walked through the kitchen door and headed to the sink to wash his hands.

CHAPTER NINE

"Y'all have a good day in school. And behave yourselves," Terrance shouted teasingly as he waved good-bye to the men filing out of the mess hall the next morning.

Assembling in pairs, the men fell in line behind Tucker and Morris for the one-mile walk that took them past two vacant company streets before they came to the long concrete apron that separated the hangers and control tower from the runway.

The airfield's main runway was just over one mile long. Tucker guessed, as he scanned the field, there were about two additional miles of short runways crisscrossing the main runway used for taxiing the planes.

Two hangars sat like matched bookends on each side of a large, two-story, cinderblock office building that also provided the foundation for the control tower.

Two cars were parked outside the office building, but unlike a few years earlier, no one was in sight.

Every day from late December 1941 to early in 1942, Pendleton Field was home to the 17th Bombardment Group. Scores of pilots, copilots, gunners, flight crews, and all of their associated support personnel filled the buildings offices and briefing rooms day and night. The Bombardment Group was assigned to fly the new North American B-25 Mitchell medium bomber on anti-submarine patrols along the coastal shipping lanes of Washington and Oregon looking for the nine Japanese submarines that were known to be there.

Shortly after Pearl Harbor was attacked, the submarines arrived in the coastal waters and began threatening American merchant ships. In a two-week period, they attacked eight ships, sinking two of them.

On Christmas Eve 1941, one of the planes with the Bombardment Group dropped four three-hundred-pound bombs on a Japanese submarine near the mouth of the Columbia River, and within a week, all of the foreign submarines disappeared from America's coastal waters.

In February 1942, the 17th Bombardment Group transferred to South Carolina, where they practiced short takeoffs and landings from an aircraft carrier for their next mission—Doolittle's raid on Tokyo.

Tucker looked down at the concrete apron in front of the building and shook his head. Cracks pockmarked with grass and weeds spidered the apron. He wondered why the army would let it deteriorate like that. He smiled when he realized it was a rhetorical question.

"If that plane isn't taken care of any better than this apron," Morris said pointing to the lone C-47 sitting outside of the next hangar, "maybe we should hope that we aren't going to be jumping,"

"The area and hangars do look a little rundown, don't they?" Tucker agreed, looking around.

Behind them, Roger elbowed Jackson and said quietly, "This place gives me the willies."

"Yeah," Jackson grimaced, "me too." He turned his head around. "What you think, Jimbo?"

"I thinks it's just fine, Jackson."

Tucker stopped at the last hangar and looked at the faded sign above the closed bay door. "Hangar A. This is us."

The large, 120-foot square hangar had been built in 1941 by the Army Corps of Engineers on a six-inch, reinforced concrete slab with concrete walls on the side and in the back. The front was left open. Wooden trusses were hand built to form a closed arch roof that was then covered with corrugated steel.

The front of the hangar was manually opened or closed by pushing five overlapping door sections hung on the top with barn door rollers.

The twenty-eight-foot by 120-foot expanse was closed when the men arrived.

Morris stepped forward and opened the exterior gray metal door on the front side of the hangar to allow Tucker to walk in.

Jackson stepped aside and turned to Jimbo. "If you think it's fine, then you go first," he said with a smile as he motioned Jimbo and Willie ahead.

"OK men quiet it down," Morris said holding the door open. "And move in smartly."

The uniformed men filed through the door in a single file and stopped inside, giving their eyes a moment to adjust to the dark, cavernous space, where at least one airplane would have typically been parked for maintenance.

No plane was there.

The men eyed each other quizzically.

"OK, men, back in pairs," Tucker said quietly when everyone was inside. He silently led them toward the lighted rear of the hangar and a small, makeshift classroom that had been set up.

As they neared, Tucker counted twenty old wooden armless chairs lined up in two rows separated by an aisle. He walked to the first row and stood at attention in front of the aisle seat, looking straight ahead at three men who were sitting behind a long gray metal table facing him: a colonel and a major in uniform, and a man in a civilian suit. A gaunt, short, blond-headed lieutenant with a large beak-like nose stood behind the three men.

Probably the colonel's aide, Tucker thought, looking at the man who was standing.

When he knew that all of the Triple Nickles were standing at attention in front of their chairs, Tucker stepped forward, looked at the colonel, and came to attention. "Captain Tucker Freeman and the men of the 555th Airborne reporting for duty, sir."

"Yes, yes," Colonel George Richardson said dismissively as he rose from his seat and motioned for the men to sit. "You may sit down." Richardson stood at five-foot-nine. He was fifty years old, but the thin wisps of gray hair on his otherwise baldhead and his thick, portly waist from too many years of sitting behind a desk made him look a decade older.

"Welcome to Pendleton Field," he began. "I'm Colonel Richardson, base commander here since 1941, when Pendleton was home to the 17th Bombardment Group—the Doolittle group that raided Tokyo," he added proudly.

That's certainly a stretch of the truth, Tucker thought, cocking his head. Tucker was a senior at West Point when Doolittle led the Tokyo Raid, and he knew that even if the group had been stationed here earlier, they had secretly trained on the East Coast for their bombing mission to Japan. He made a mental note to find out more about it later and then raised his hand and waited for Richardson's acknowledgement, "Sir, what units are stationed here now?"

Richardson glared at Tucker for a long moment, obviously uncomfortable with the question. "An engineering unit, a support unit..." He paused as he looked from Tucker to the other men in front of him, "...and you."

Tucker realized that Pendleton Field wasn't considered a working base any longer. *It's just a shell,* he thought, *and he doesn't have anyone to command. This will certainly make life interesting.*

"The two people beside me," Richardson continued, "are temporarily assigned here as instructors. Major Charles Wesley—" Richardson motioned toward a thirty-five-year-old, slender man with wavy brown hair sitting on his immediate left, "—is a bomb disposal instructor and the military head of this special program. And Doctor Bill Silva—" He motioned toward the dark-haired civilian wearing black-rimmed glasses and sitting on the other side of the major, "—is a firefighting expert on loan from the Forest Service."

Wesley and Silva nodded toward the men.

"You only need to remember one thing, and we'll get along just fine: you're going to be working with Major Wesley and Doctor Silva, but I'm the CO of Pendleton Field and I'm in charge." Richardson walked to the end of the table. "If you need anything at this base, you are to see me," he said, looking directly at Tucker. "My office is in the cinderblock building under the control tower. Just make an appointment with my secretary." He paused for a moment, and the lieutenant standing behind the table coughed loudly. "Oh, yes," Richardson continued, "We have some other business—housekeeping, if you will—to take care of."

He walked forward and stopped in front of Tucker's chair. Almost toe to toe, he looked down and said, "My aide, Lieutenant Davis, tells me that someone assigned you colored officers to the BOQ." The lieutenant stood up straighter and looked at Tucker, smiling as Richardson continued. "That building is slated to be closed, so I think it would be better if you moved out of there—today."

The game is on, Tucker thought. He stood quickly and came to attention. "We'll move out—today, sir."

Richardson, who was four inches shorter than Tucker, was forced to look up. He stepped back and Tucker sat down.

Wesley and Silva exchanged a discrete smile. After being around the colonel for over a week, they both knew he was insecure and arrogant, and he didn't like the idea of the Triple Nickles being on *his* base.

But it looked like the captain could hold his own.

Richardson turned to Davis. "Lieutenant, please go by the BOQ at 1700 to make sure it's locked."

"Yes sir," Davis said as his skinny frame snapped to attention.

Richardson walked back to the table and leaned straight-armed on his fists, looking at the group of men sitting in front of him. "You men have been assigned to Company Street R with the service unit. The rest of the base personnel reside on Company Streets A, B, and C, or in the private housing adjacent to those streets." He stood up straight and slowly looked from man to man. "There is no reason for any of you to be in that area... ever." He paused and then walked to the side of the table again. "And, lastly, the base mess hall..."

His words were interrupted by the sound of the metal side door opening, followed a moment later by the sound of high heels quickly tapping across the cement floor on their way to the classroom area.

When a young woman finally appeared in the lighted area, Tucker saw that she was in her mid-twenties, five-foot-four, and thin. Her milk-white face was topped by short, curly blond hair that bounced with every tap of her brown and white Oxford high heels as she hurried past the men to the front of the classroom.

"Sorry to interrupt, Colonel," Hazel Howell said, fanning herself with her fingers when she reached the table, "but there's some general on the phone that needs to talk to you." The gum in her mouth popped when she said the last word, punctuating the end of her sentence like a verbal period. "Sorry," she said shyly as she put her right hand in front of her bright red lips.

Richardson stared at her in disbelief. "Did you leave him hanging on the phone?"

"Yeah," she answered sweetly. "Did you want me to hang up on him?"

Richardson moved closer. "You should have told him that I was in a meeting and I'd call him back."

"OK, I can still do that." Hazel crossed her arms across her chest. "So you want me to go back and tell him you're too busy to talk to him now? You'll call him back."

"Sir," Lieutenant Davis stepped forward, "shall I take care of this?"

Hazel glared at Davis and dropped her arms. "I am perfectly capable of telling the general that the colonel is busy and will have to call him back, Lieutenant." She pursed her lips and turned brusquely to leave.

"Hazel, stop right there!" Richardson barked. "I'll take the call." He picked his cap up from the table and turned to Wesley. "Carry on, Major."

"Yes, sir."

Tucker and his men stood and came to attention as Richardson, clearly upset, walked briskly past them heading for the door with Davis following three steps behind. A moment later, the metal door shut with a loud clank.

Wesley motioned the men to sit down.

Hazel looked from Wesley to Silva, and in a voice that sounded stronger and more professional than it had just moments before, she said, "Sorry, I couldn't get here any sooner." She took the gum out of her mouth, wrapped it in a small piece of paper she picked up from the table, and then lobbed the wad toward the trashcan at the other side of the table. It went in. "Two points," she said with a smile, winking at Silva.

"I'm Hazel Howell, Colonel Richardson's secretary," she said, turning to Tucker. "Welcome to Pendleton Field, Captain. If you ever need help with anything, I'm the first person you'll see in the colonel's office." She offered her hand.

Tucker looked at Hazel and her outstretched hand. After a long moment, he reached out and quickly shook it. "Captain Tucker Freemen, ma'am. And," he swept his arm out toward the rest of the platoon, "the men of the 555th Airborne." The men nodded toward Hazel.

"It's a pleasure to meet all of you," she said with a broad smile. "I'm sure we'll be seeing a lot more of each other." She waved over her shoulder to Wesley and Silva as she turned and headed to the door, her heels once again tapping out every step on the cement hangar floor and echoing in the vast openness.

Major Wesley slid his chair back from the metal table and stood. "Well, now that the introductions are over and you've met two of the most important people you'll have to deal with at Pendleton Field," he said with a smile, "let's get down to business, shall we."

He took a moment to look at the men in front of him and then began. "You're here because the army thinks you're the best men for a classified mission they've code named 'Operation Firefly.'" He picked up a three-foot wooden pointer from the table and walked toward a map of the Pacific Ocean, tacked on one of the two cork-boards behind him. "Our country is under attack by the Japanese." Wesley touched the tip of the pointer to Japan before he continued. "According to our intelligence people, during the last six months, the Japanese have launched thousands of large balloons—called Fu-Gos—from the northern coast of Japan.

"The balloon is attached to a metal ring with a box of equipment, sitting on a smaller ring, which we call the gondola, above it. Hanging down from the ring there's either an antipersonnel bomb or a couple of incendiary bombs—sometimes both.

"The balloons are filled with hydrogen gas, so when they're released the Fu-Gos climb to about thirty thousand feet into what the meteorologists call a high, atmospheric wind stream. They are carried by that wind stream eastward across the ocean." He used the pointer to trace a path from Japan up the western rim of the Pacific across the North Pacific and then down the west coast of North America. "To date, Fu-Gos have been spotted on Alaska's mainland, along the Aleutian Islands, and as far north as St. Lawrence Island in the Bering Sea. In Canada, they've landed in British Columbia, Alberta, Saskatchewan, and as far east as Manitoba. In the US, while the main concentration has been in Washington,

Oregon, California, Idaho, and Montana, they've also been spotted as far east as Iowa."

Wesley turned from the map and set his pointer on the table. "The army's been able to retrieve a couple dozen of intact Fu-Gos and a lot of fragments and bits of equipment from ones that have exploded." He paused letting the last word hang in the air before he continued. "For the last three months I've been stationed at a base in California where I've been working with a team of military and civilian experts examining and analyzing every fragment of gondola or armament that's been brought in. And while many hundreds of balloon bombs have been sited, only a couple hundred have made it to our shores, so far. But unfortunately, one of them was responsible for the six deaths that were just reported by the newspapers." He moved toward the map again.

Tucker raised his hand.

"Yes, Captain."

"How can this mission be classified if it's been in the paper?"

"That's a very good question." Wesley grimaced and began pacing. "As I'm sure you can understand, the army tried to keep the existence of the Japanese Fu-Gos program under a pretty tight wrap—the psychological impact would be devastating to the general public to know we're under attack by paper balloons from Japan. Plus the army didn't want the Japanese to know that they were scaring the bejeebies out of us."

He stopped and turned to the men. "But when innocent Americans died, the department knew we'd be remiss if we didn't go public with information about the Fu-Gos, and warn them how potentially dangerous—lethal—the bombs can be."

He walked to the front of the table. "So, why is this mission classified?" He paused to take a deep breath before he continued. "Because the whole story still isn't out. We also know that the Japs have chemical and biological agents, like anthrax. And, as they demonstrated in China, they're not afraid to use them. That's one of the things that's got us worried." He began pacing again. "We haven't seen any evidence that they are using chemicals or biologicals, so far, but that's why we're thoroughly checking everything we can recover."

Wesley glanced at Silva and then back at the men and continued. "One of the greatest danger we're facing is actually from forest fires. The incendiaries the Fu-Gos carry have ignited hundreds of square miles of forests and destroyed thousands of acres of valuable timber. To defend against these attacks, we…no, you…will have to learn to use new equipment…equipment that is virtually untested. And you'll need to follow some new procedures…ones that look good on the drawing board, but to be perfectly honest, haven't actually been tried yet."

The men turned exchanging apprehensive looks.

Wesley moved a portable corkboard to the front and tacked on a large drawing of one of the Japanese balloons with a large antipersonnel and four incendiary bombs hanging from its metal-ringed gondola.

"Your primary mission is to disarm these," Wesley said as he pointed to the bombs. "But you will also need to be prepared to fight fires the incendiary bombs may start—which they've proved they will do." He looked back at the men. "And we'll also be asking you to retrieve any intact balloons or bombs or fragments."

Tucker immediately raised his hand, "Sir, why isn't the army using one of their bomb disposal units?"

Wesley walked back to a map that showed a topographic view of North America's west coast. "As you can see here," he said, pointing at a series of colored dots concentrated in the vast coastal mountain ranges, "most of the balloons that have been sited are in pretty remote heavily forested areas." He looked back at the men. "We've got two thousand seven hundred troops stationed at critical points in the coastal states ready to move in and fight grass and forest fires from the ground, anywhere there's access. What the army—and the Forest Service—really need are people who can parachute into the remote areas when a balloon is sighted." He looked back at Tucker, "And the army decided it would be faster for you to learn to defuse Fu-Gos than for a bomb unit to learn to parachute."

Tucker's men let out a collective sigh.

Morris raised his hand, "But, Major, we were taught to pick nice open, flat areas to parachute into...not forests!"

"Right." Wesley nodded his head and smiled. "Remember me mentioning new techniques? That was army code for teaching you to find the softest treetop available."

The men didn't laugh.

Wesley walked back to the table and stood next to Silva. "During the next two weeks, I'm going to teach you how to disarm or destroy Fu-Gos, while Doctor Silva and his Forest Service team train you to fight fires and to..." He put his hand on Silva's shoulder and asked, "What was that name you guys are using, Bill?"

"Smoke jump," Silva answered.

"Smoke jump," Wesley repeated, looking pointedly at the men seated in front of him. "You're about to become bomb defusers, firefighters, and smoke jumpers." Wesley waited to let the words sink in before he continued.

"Sir," Tucker raised his hand, "how are we ever supposed to do all of that from here? That's thousands of miles to cover."

"Right." Wesley nodded. "But you're no longer a *test platoon.* Another detachment of the 555th will be arriving in Chico, California, next week to start the same training program at the Chico Army Airfield. They're going to cover northern California and southern Oregon, and depending on the situation, they may be called here to help you, or you may be sent to California for a fire."

The men sitting in the wooden chairs smiled for the first time in days. There were more Triple Nickles.

"OK," Wesley continued, "let's get started by talking about some of that new equipment I mentioned earlier."

He held up a three-foot-long canvas duffel bag with parachute webbing straps. "You learned all about these A-5 Aerial Delivery Containers in jump school, so this bag's not new to you. But you probably also learned to pack them with ammo boxes and weapons—the things infantry paratroopers need on the ground. What you're going to learn to pack in A-5s now are the things you'll need for your new mission: defusing tools, gas masks, shovels, and this—the Pulaski," Wesley said handing a hand tool that combined an axe and an adze in one head to Doctor Silva.

Silva pushed his chair back, stood up and took over. "This tool was invented by a Forest Service ranger—Ed

Pulaski—in 1911, and I'll guarantee that it's the best, most versatile tool you'll ever use to dig or to chop, and it's especially good for making firebreaks," he said as he turned to Wesley. "As a matter of fact, if it's OK with the major, I'd like to plan on going outside tomorrow morning to show you how to make a firebreak, and to teach you some other basic firefighting techniques you're going to need to know."

Wesley nodded.

"Great," Silva continued. "I've always thought that you learn a lot more by doing than by watching." He looked at his watch and then turned to Tucker. "It's almost lunch time and I imagine you could use a little time to get resettled, so unless you have any questions, why don't we call it a day, and get an early start tomorrow."

Wesley looked at the men. "Questions?"

When no one spoke, Wesley stood, "OK then, we'll meet here at 0700. Have a good evening. We've got a full day planned for tomorrow."

The men stood and came to attention in front of their chairs.

"Dismissed," Wesley said. He rolled up maps that were lying on the table as he watched the men file quietly out of the hangar.

He turned to Silva. "So what do you think about our new jumpers," he asked when he heard the metal door close.

"I think that they're going to do fine—no, actually I think they're going to do better than fine," Silva answered with a smile.

"I agree. We've got a lot of work to cram into the next couple of weeks, but I think we're going to have one hellava team when we're done!"

CHAPTER TEN

Morris parked *Lucille* in front of the barracks.

"It's certainly not the BOQ," Tucker said as he grabbed his Valpak and headed to the barracks door.

"No, it's not," Morris said with a perfunctory nod as he grabbed his bag, "but I'll sure be a lot more comfortable here than I was there last night."

I won't, Tucker thought, reaching for the screen door.

"Atten-hut!" Boyle's voice boomed from inside.

The barracks had the same layout as the ones they'd lived in at Mackall and Fort Benning—an NCO room on each side of the front door, nineteen beds in the squad room, and a shower room in the back with latrines, sinks, and showers. And, following army edict, the beds toward the back that weren't being used by the platoon, had their bare mattresses folded in half exposing their metal springs.

"As you were, men," Tucker said, looking around. "Since we're going to be bunking together, let's just keep it informal as the lieutenant and I come and go."

The men quickly broke up into their small groups, leaving Boyle, Sawyer, and Roger standing next to Tucker and Morris.

"Let me take your bag," Sawyer said as he stepped forward and reached for Tucker's Valpak.

Roger took Morris's bag from his shoulder. "We have our two swankiest rooms ready for you, sirs." He pointed to the NCO rooms. "The captain is in the Savoy, on the right." Then he gestured to the room on the left. "And the lieutenant in the Apollo.

Morris turned to Boyle. "I thought that was your room, Sarge."

"Was." He gave a rueful laugh. "I decided to move out here so I could keep a closer eye on the men."

Sawyer and Roger groaned at the comment and then picked up the bags and moved them to the NCO rooms.

Both rooms were ten feet by ten feet with a wide, narrow window that sat high on the outside wall. The single bedstead in each room had a painted, curved aluminum headboard and footboard connected by an arched rail frame with link-meshed springs. The felted cotton mattress was covered with two white cotton sheets and a green sixty-six-by-eighty-four-inch wool army-issued blanket with *US* printed in large letters centered squarely in the middle of the bed. The bottom corners of the blanket were mitered "hospital style" at a perfect forty-five-degree angle and ready for inspection.

Sawyer took Tucker's extra uniforms out of his Valpak and hung them on a row of wooden pegs along the wall.

"Would you like me to put the rest of your things in your dresser, Captain?"

"No, that's OK. It'll give me something to do."

"Is there anything else I can get for you?" Sawyer asked.

Tucker looked around—it wasn't the BOQ, but there wasn't anything Sawyer could do about that. "No. But thank you for your help, Corporal."

Sawyer nodded and left. He joined Dixie, who was leaning against the wall by the front door fingering his saxophone.

"Hey, Dix, I'm in the mood for a little music...what you got?" Sawyer asked as he opened his trumpet case. He wasn't close to being the musician that Dixie was, but as long as he didn't play louder than Dixie, no one minded his occasional slightly off-key notes.

Dixie blew warm air into his hands, rubbed them together, and finally answered, "Let's try 'Tin Roof Blues.'"

Sawyer nodded and fingered the three keys on his trumpet, waiting on Dixie.

Dixie looked at Willie. "Come on, Willie," he finally called, "you know I can't do this without you and the bird."

Willie wrinkled his nose at Dixie as he grabbed the army-issued red fire bucket from the front door and two drumsticks from his locker. He sat down beside Sawyer, and with Angel on his shoulder followed Dixie's lead, playing rhythm.

One by one the rest of the men found comfortable places to sit and listen to the trio.

Boyle watched and listened from a chair in the corner. "Now this is something no white boys, or Uncle Tom, can take away from us!" He said to no one in particular as he leaned back in his chair and smiled.

PART 3: THE SMOKE JUMPERS

CHAPTER ELEVEN

The bright morning light streamed through the open hangar bay door reflecting off the twenty-eight-foot, white nylon parachute canopy spread out on the concrete floor.

"I think you're going to really like using these new parachutes a lot more than your army ones," Silva enthusiastically told the group of men gathered around the parachute. "They're called Derry parachutes, and were designed by Frank Derry, an instructor and trainer at our Missoula headquarters. What makes them perfect for the job," Silva continued as he pointed to the two vertical slit openings on each side of the canopy, "are these: Derry Slots. They'll give you maneuverability."

"Sir, are you telling us that we'll be jumping using a parachute that has two seams that ain't sewed all the way?" Roger asked skeptically. "Has anyone tried them yet?"

Tucker scowled at Roger. "Corporal, the army wouldn't ask us to test an untested Forest Service parachute."

"Well, it wouldn't surprise me a bit," Boyle said quietly as he looked from Roger to Jackson then Dixie.

"The captain is right," Silva grinned. "Frank Derry, his brother Chet, and other firefighters in Missoula have been using these parachutes for about a year now, and they all agree—the parachute is not only safe, it's steerable. And that's something that's especially important when you're jumping into rugged terrain and forests."

"I guess we'll see," Boyle retorted.

"Yes, you will, Sergeant," Major Wesley said, startling Boyle when he and a captain walked up from behind to join the group. "Your two-week training program has officially started, and I want you to do three jumps today. The first two will be here at the base. They'll give you a chance to try out your new 'chutes and learn how to maneuver them. Then we'll go to Wallowa Forest just east of here." He looked at his watch. "You take off in an hour, so I thought you should meet the man who will pilot your C-47 jumps—Captain Jonathan Jones, call sign Jonesy. He spent the last month working with smoke jumpers in Missoula, and the year before that he was in the CBI—China, Burma, India theater."

Jonesy looked at the men and nodded. He was thirty-two, six feet tall, thin and clean-shaven. He was wearing a flight suit and a dark-brown leather jacket with a large, dyed leather patch, known as a Blood Chit, sewn on the back. Across the top of the patch, a US flag sat next to a Chinese nationalist flag. The large white space on the bottom contained the Chinese characters for the words that downed aviators considered their last hope: *This foreign person has come to China to help in the war effort. Soldiers and civilians, one and all, should rescue, protect, and provide him with medical care.*

After more than sixty mission of flying cargo across "the Hump"—the Himalayan mountain range between India and China—Jonesy was downed. When he got back to his base in India, his army detailer told him about

Pendleton Field, and he took it without hesitating as soon as he learned that the base had has favorite plane: a C-47. He'd hoped that working with the Forest Service would be an interesting assignment, and after a month in Missoula, he knew he'd made the right decision.

Wesley turned to Silva. "Set the men up with a new 'chute, and have two more 'chutes per man ready."

Silva nodded.

Wesley looked at Jonesy and the rest of the men. "OK. Two practice jumps here at the airfield. Then you'll fly up to Shone Canyon for the third jump, so you can practice finding those soft tree tops I told you about," he said, smiling.

"Don't listen to him," Silva chimed in. "You'll be able to use your new 'chutes to steer away from most of the tree tops." Then added with a shrug, "But if you don't, you have your let-down rope. We have to use them all the time around Missoula. Just remember the knots we practiced this morning. Especially the half hitches, slip knot, and the all-important rabbit—it comes *up* the hole, runs *around* the tree, and goes back *down* the hole."

The men began to chuckle.

"I think you get it," Silva continued. "OK, there's an old logging road in the area where you'll be jumping—consider that your drop zone and try to land near it. After you pick up your 'chutes, just follow the road down the canyon to an old log cabin—it's one of our old Forest Service buildings. I'll arrange for a truck to meet you there to give you a ride back."

The men nodded.

"And remember," Silva added, "don't leave anything behind—no gear, no trash. What you take in, you bring out. We need to keep our forests clean."

Jonesy looked at Wesley. "If you'll excuse me, sir, I'll go get the plane ready." Wesley nodded and Jonesy gave him a casual salute as he headed for the door.

"OK. Assignments," Wesley said looking at Silva. "I'll stay here and coordinate from the tower. Silva, you're jump master. I want the men to jump in two teams of eight. The drop zone is the runway outside the hangar." Wesley turned to the men and continued. "As soon as you land and get your 'chute off, come back here and get a new chute. I want everyone outside ready to take off again when the plane comes back around and lands."

He paused for a moment. "Captain, you jump with the second team, and I want you to copilot until then."

"Yes, sir," Tucker replied.

"Second jump, Morris you take copilot."

Morris nodded.

"And for the third jump," he said looking around, "Sawyer, you're copilot."

Sawyer stood straighter, "Yes, sir," he answered, smiling.

"That'll make five of us who will start getting experience to help Jonesy. If he ever needs our help. Or just to handle the radio." Wesley turned to Tucker. "That reminds me, I want to get Terrance familiar with the tower, especially the communications radio. We'll probably need him up there for most of our flights."

"I'll tell him when we finish today, sir."

Wesley nodded. "OK, men, let's get ready."

"Holy baseplate," Roger exclaimed as he staggered through the screen door of the barracks. "I thought we were just gonna do one jump in that canyon. I can't believe the major found time for us to do a second one. I ain't never fell into and out of that many trees in my whole life."

"I hear you," Jackson agreed. "I got bruises on my bruises, and my brain's still swimming from when I hit my head on the first jump."

"Well, since you ain't got much of a brain, it shouldn't be swimming for long," Boyle offered.

"Thanks, Sarge," Jackson said, rubbing the back of his neck.

"I hit my head a couple of good ones too. Plus a goddamn tree branch just about poked my eye out." Sawyer added. "I think we need to be wearing our football helmets instead of them wimpy army caps."

From his room, Tucker listened to the men recount their first day's jump as he was getting out his toiletries for a hot shower. He stopped mid-motion when he heard Sawyer's comment. A moment later, he put the toiletries down, walked out to the Squad Room, and stopped in front of Sawyer.

"That's actually a great idea," he said.

Sawyer looked at Tucker with a quizzical look trying to remember what he could have said that was a good idea.

Tucker smiled. "Wearing our football helmets." He looked around at the other men. "Why not? They're designed to protect our heads. Why not wear them to jump?"

Boyle stepped up. "Because they're not army-issued? They ain't ever gonna let us do that," he answered smugly.

"The Derby parachute isn't army-issued," Tucker shot back, then turned to the rest of the men. "Let's take them tomorrow. I'll talk to Silva and Major Wesley."

Tucker patted Sawyer's back. "That really was a brilliant idea, Corporal."

"The army'll never approve it," Boyle said quietly to Jackson and Roger as he walked to the back of the squad room to the showers.

Roger shook his head and whispered to Jackson. "A helmet probably wouldn't help him anyway. I think he's been dropped on his head too many times already."

CHAPTER TWELVE

For the next week, the training was led by an intelligence officer, Major Steven Hale, a Fu-Go expert who had worked with Major Wesley as part of the California-based Army team.

Hale brought mock-ups of the different types of incendiary and high explosive anti-personnel bombs that had been found and brought to the team. He also had several gondola rings with fuses, aneroids, igniter squibs, and the other component pieces the men needed to familiarize themselves with for defusing bombs.

He and Wesley started their training in the classroom and finished it in the hills and valleys around Pendleton Field where they placed bombs in trees, tall grass fields and even barbed wire fences for the teams of men to find and defuse.

When the teams arrived back in the hangar after defusing and retrieving three gondolas, incendiary and anti-personal bombs each, Jackson raised his hand and asked Hale which team had defused the live bomb he'd said was out there.

"Actually they should have all been live—in your minds. And since everyone is back, you all passed your final exam, with flying colors." Wesley and Hale exchanged smiles

"Did he just say that they was all live?" Roger asked Jackson quietly.

"I'm not sure." They both shrugged.

For the second week of training, Doctor Silva brought in a Forest Service team from their headquarters in Missoula to teach the Triple Nickles how to fight forest fires and prevent them from spreading. But although the fire season had started, there weren't fires in the area, so the men practiced jumping with their new gear, then using the tools to make practice firebreaks. By the end of the week they had expanded the fire trails in nearby Kassy's Canyon by several miles.

Their final test included five jump sites selected by Silva for their fire potential and their extreme terrain conditions ranging from dense forests to craggy mountains.

When the men walked down the fire road after their fifth jump, Wesley and Silva knew that the men were ready.

The two-week training program concluded.

"I want you to know that you all really impressed the Forest Service team," Silva told the men sitting in the classroom for the debriefing after their last jump. "Your idea to wear football helmets was brilliant. And Forest Service headquarters has taken it on. They're working with a Montana company to redesign the front guard piece, and when they're finished we're going to issue them as part of the smoke jumpers standard equipment."

Jackson and Roger smacked Sawyer's red head.

"Ain't you something," Jackson teased.

"Brilliant, that's what I am, brilliant," Sawyer answered as he puffed out his chest.

"Geeze." The rest of the men shook their heads and moaned in unison,

Major Wesley stood up. "Well, as long as we're handing out accolades for brilliance, I think Private Brown—Jimbo—deserves the army's gratitude for his idea to hook up a speaker system next to the jump door."

Jimbo smiled shyly and nodded at the recognition.

Wesley continued, "I doubt the army will buy the idea as quickly as the Forest Service bought into the helmet idea, but nonetheless, I've seen firsthand how helpful it is for the jumpmaster and the jumpers. So on behalf of the army, I thank you."

The men patted Jimbo on the back and his face lit up with a big grin. "I had a feeling it would be useful."

"Good Lord," Boyle said shaking his head, "Sawyer and Jimbo. Now there's two heads that won't be able to fit through Betty's door tonight."

CHAPTER THIRTEEN

Betty Stone opened her bar at precisely five o'clock everyday except Sundays and kept it open as long as there were paying customers, and her two waitresses were willing to work.

Following her normal routine, at 4:59 p.m. Betty sauntered over to the front door, unlocked it and flipped the "Closed" sign to "Open", then she'd walk back to her stool behind the bar to rest what she described as her "two hundred pounds of chocolate love".

When Betty saw the Ebenezer Baptist Church bus pull up, she grabbed the tube of Revlon's Bright Forecast lipstick she kept next to the cash register, leaned toward the mirror and applied the vivid red color to her full lips. She adjusted the peroxide blond finger waves that pushed down her forehead and, lastly, did one final check to make sure there wasn't any red lipstick on her pearly white teeth. Satisfied, she turned around just as her first customers were rushing through the door heading for their favorite tables.

"Evening, Betty," Willie and Jimbo said in unison as they grabbed one of the tables near the bar.

"Evening, boys." Betty smiled. She grabbed six brown glass bottles of Pioneer beer from the ice chest, opened them, and lined them up on the bar. When she had a dozen bottles opened, she called the two waitresses, "Mable, Sadie, cold ones up."

Both waitresses were in their early twenty and had worked for Betty since they were in high school, and although they were her nieces neither of them had inherited Betty's girth. Mable had olive skin, green eyes and as her mother described her, she was thin and straight as a broom handle.

Sadie was two inches shorter than Mable, had the same olive skin, bright brown eyes and a body that was perfectly curved exactly where it needed to be—above and below her thin waist.

Mable hurried to the bar, grabbed six beers and set down two orders. "Two turkey dinners, four steaks, and I need two Coca-Cola's."

Betty picked up the orders and looked at them with a smile, "Can always tell when it's payday!" She turned to Sadie, "What you got, honey?"

"Six steaks, so far," she answered as she set her orders down and picked up the six remaining open beers. "And I need eight more beers."

"Good Lord almighty, it's gonna be one of them nights." Betty opened the beers and set them on the counter before disappearing through the kitchen door with her fist full of orders.

Sadie carried two beers to the end of the bar and handed one to Boyle and the other one to Dixie. "Your dinner'll be out shortly."

Boyle took a long swig of his beer, then held up the bottle, "That's fine, Sadie. You just keep these coming in the meantime, OK, Sugar?"

Sadie looked at Dixie and rolled her eyes.

He shook his head and shrugged his shoulders. *Boyle is just being Boyle.*

Boyle swiveled his seat around and smiled broadly as he watched Sadie walk away. "She sure is sweet." His face suddenly turned to a scowl. Tucker and Morris walked in and sat down at a table near the door. He turned back to Dixie, lit a cigarette and asked, "What do you suppose Uncle Tom's doing here?"

Dixie turned his head to see what Boyle was looking at. "Looks like the Captain is having a beer with the Lieutenant," he answered waving Boyle's smoke away from his face.

"Naw. More likely he's waiting for us to mess up."

Dixie stared at Boyle for a long moment, and then stood up. "Then spoil his fun and don't get drunk for a change." He picked up his beer, saw Jimbo and Willie drinking colas at a nearby table, and walked away from the bar toward them.

"Mind if I join you?" Dixie asked Willie.

"Sure. I was just telling Jimbo how good Angel did today. She got back to her box twenty minutes after I released her. You know not every bird can adjust to a new area that quick," he said proudly. "She sure is special."

Dixie sighed and took a long swig of his beer.

Sawyer leaned toward Dixie from the next table. "Hey, Dix, why don't you join us?" He called above the building noise.

Dixie turned around to talk to Sawyer and saw Roger and Jackson teasing Mable and Sadie unmercifully. He shook his head as he watch the two men try to get the girls to sit on their laps and join them for a beer. "Thanks, but it doesn't look like y'all need any more company," he finally answered Sawyer.

Jimbo turned his head to see what all of the ruckus was about at the next table, then shook his head. "I don't think Miss Lulu or Miss Billie would like them acting that way."

"I don't think so either," Dixie agreed as he stood up. "Y'all need another cola?"

"Sure, thanks Dixie," Willie replied. "And one for Jimbo, too."

Dixie turned to the next table and added loudly, "I'm going to the bar to grab two colas and a beer, since the waitresses are too busy to do their job." When he turned and took a step he collided with Terrance, almost knocking him over. "Sorry, Terrance."

"My fault, I wasn't paying attention."

Dixie turned his head and saw Betty smiling and ogling Terrance from the bar.

"Oh. I understand." He smiled and sat back down at the table. "Looks like Betty's busy too. I think I'll just wait on that beer."

Willie and Jimbo followed his gaze and then nodded in agreement.

"Yeah, I still got a little cola," Willie said, smiling.

"I'm sorry I'm late, sugar," Terrance said sweetly as he grabbed a stool and sat down across the bar from Betty.

"I wasn't worried, honey, I knew you'd be along," Betty cooed back and covered his hand with hers. "So what can I get for you tonight?" She said mischievously, not noticing that Boyle had moved next to Terrance.

"Well, you can get me some change for the jukebox," Boyle interjected as he put a dollar bill on the counter. "We need to get this place jumping."

Betty's broad smile turned to a scowl as she turned her squinting eyes from Terrance to Boyle. "No jukebox tonight, Sergeant," she told him curtly. "I got some musicians coming in. They'll be playing shortly. So why don't you go and sit down?"

Boyle's face scowled back at Betty letting her know that he wasn't happy. He pushed his dollar forward. "Then how about another beer?"

"Sure." Betty opened a Pioneer, set in on the counter, and took Boyle's money. Without taking her eyes off Boyle, she put it in the cash register drawer and shut it.

"Don't I get change, Betty?" He asked gruffly.

"I've put the change on your account," she answered smugly. "Just in case you get drunk and forget to pay me, again."

Boyle opened his mouth to say something, but stopped when Betty pursed her bright red lips and crossed her arms across her ample chest, glaring at him.

He turned to Terrance. "I don't know how you put up with her." He picked up his beer and headed back to the other end of the bar.

"He's something, ain't he?" Terrance asked as he shook his head. "Ain't never satisfied unless he gets the last word."

Betty watched Boyle go. "Well, I ain't letting him put a mood on me." She put her sweetest face back on and leaned on the bar in front of Terrance. "You wanna stay tonight, honey?" She smiled coyly, and added, "I could use some loving."

"I gotta be at work real early tomorrow, sugar."

Betty straightened up, and Terrance watched her smile fade.

"Believe me, I'm sorry, sugar," he said quickly. "Maybe we could sneak upstairs for awhile?" He asked with a smile.

Betty looked at him and arched her left eyebrow. "Well, honey, I ain't got no time to be sneaking around." She turned and slowly sashayed to the kitchen. "I gots to work, too." She nodded her head over her shoulder to punctuate the sentence, and then disappeared through the kitchen door.

"Damn you woman, why you got to be like that?" Terrance called after her.

Sadie walked behind the bar, opened three beers, and gave Terrance a smug look that let him know she was on Betty's side.

"Mind your own business you little hussy, and stay out of mine," Terrance said, grabbing one of the beers as she walked by.

She harrumphed and kept walking.

Tucker slowly sipped his beer from a table next to the door, and watched as Sadie set a beer down in front of Roger, then set herself down on his lap, while Jackson fawned over Mabel. "Now there's trouble waiting to happen," Tucker said as he turned to Morris. "Their wives are in town, right? At the same rooming house as Pearl?"

"Yup. They told their wives that they had to supervise the men tonight, so they couldn't spend the evening with them." Morris looked at the pair carrying on with the waitresses, and shook his head. "But somehow Lulu Roger always knows what's goin' on. Pearl said the ladies are..."

He stopped midsentence when the door next to their table pushed opened and a short, plump woman wearing a summer dress and a large white hat walked in and looked around.

"Julius Roger," Lulu crossed her arms and barked, "looks to me like you're the one that needs supervising tonight."

Billie Jackson walked in the door behind Lulu, and crossed her arms over her tall, thin frame. "Lonnie Jackson, you best get your hands on the table where I can see them."

Mable and Sadie looked at Roger and Jackson then stood up and scurried off.

Side by side, Lulu and Billie stomped over to the table where their husbands were sitting with their heads hanging low.

"Lulu…this is a surprise," Roger said finally looking up.

"So was what I just saw."

Sawyer stood and offered his chair to Lulu while he pulled out another chair for Billie. They both sat down in a huff staring at their husbands. Sawyer turned and quietly walked away leaving the two couples alone at the table.

"Awww baby, we was just enjoying one beer," Roger said then looked at Jackson. "Then me and Jackson was gonna come to Miss Rae's to get you two."

Jackson nodded, agreeing.

"Umm-hmm." Lulu said as she put her purse on the table. "Do we really look that stupid?"

Neither Roger nor Jackson answered.

Billie looked at her husband and smiled. "Jackson, how 'bout you call one of your floozies over and order me and Lulu a beer."

"Sure thing, sweetheart." Jackson caught Sadie's attention, held up two fingers, and pointed to Billie and Lulu. Sadie nodded, grabbed two beers from the bar, and set them on the table without looking at anyone or saying a word.

Suddenly a loud whistle reverberated through the noisy din in the room.

Everyone turned and Betty, with two fingers pressed between her lips, whistled again. "Quiet down!" The bar got quiet immediately and Betty continued. "I got a real treat for y'all tonight. We got musicians that are gonna play for us."

A beautiful slim Negro woman in her early twenties carrying a fiddle, and two tall, thin young Negro men one with a guitar and the other with a banjo appeared beside Betty.

Betty put her large, bare arm around the young woman, "The Water Drops are on their way to California, and I offered to let them stay with me for a couple of days in exchange for playing some ole time Negro music for us this evening."

Everyone in the bar clapped.

"OK, OK," Betty said quieting the room again, "let's push these tables back and make room for dancing, 'cause your feet won't be able to sit still once they start playing."

The Water Drops grabbed three chairs for themselves and huddled in a corner tuning their instruments while the men in the bar began rearranging the rest of the tables and chairs.

When they were done, the young woman stood up and looked around. "Got your dancing shoes on?" She asked loudly.

The audience whistled and clapped.

"OK. Well we're gonna start the night with "*Cornbread and Butterbeans.*"

Tucker leaned toward Morris. "I grew up listening to my grandfather play that tune on his harmonica. That man could do everything."

Morris smiled. "My grandfather was perfect too…as I remember him!" He stood up, put his empty beer bottle down and grabbed his cap from the table. "Thanks for the beer, Captain. I hate to leave, but I've got plans for a quiet evening—alone with my wife. I'll be back at the barracks by 0530."

"Sounds good. Would you mind dropping me off at the gas station just past Miss Mae's? There are two lovely ladies back in DC. I promised to call this week."

"Two?" Morris raised his right eyebrow and gave Tucker an impressed smiled.

Tucker took the wallet out of his uniform breast pocket and opened it to show Morris a photograph of two very beautiful, elegantly dressed women. "My two ladies. Dorothy—my fiancée and Emma Freeman—my mother."

Morris looked at the photo and smiled. "Beautiful. Both of them."

Tucker nodded and picked his cap up from the table. The two men headed for the door just as the trio of musicians began to stomp their feet and play their lively rendition of "*Cornbread and Butterbeans*."

CHAPTER FOURTEEN

Tired from their long night at Betty's, the ragtag group of men slowly dragged themselves into the hangar and found their seats.

Boyle was the last one through the door and sat in the row behind Roger and Jackson

"Wasn't that something, Lulu and Billie showin' up at Betty's last night," he said loudly to no one in particular. "I sure wish I would've had a camera." He slapped his knee and laughed. "I ain't never seen so much white in a nigger's eyes."

Jackson and Roger moaned in unison, but didn't turn around.

Willie, who was sitting next to Boyle, turned and said. "Well, Sarge, I think it was mighty nice that they came."

"Me too," Jimbo agreed, leaning in front of Willie to talk to Boyle. "That Miss Lulu sure do have a knack for knowin' everything that's goin' on, don't she?" He paused for a moment, and then added sincerely, "I thinks she's a seer, too."

Boyle slapped his knee and started laughing again.

Roger turned around to say something to Boyle, but stopped when he saw Wesley and Silva walking toward the group. He grimaced at Boyle and turned back around.

Wesley moved quickly to the front table, handed a rolled up map to Doctor Silva then turned and looked at the men. "Good morning. We just got word of a lightening strike fire about fifty miles from here in the Wallowa National Forest."

Silva rolled a corkboard toward the men, pinned up the map, and picked up the pointer taking over. "The fire is in this area," he said circling a narrow valley between two long mountain ranges running north to south on the map. "A road forms a natural firebreak across the northern valley, so the Forest Service has two teams of firefighters southwest of the fire—one team is making a firebreak along the base of the western mountain to try and stop the fire from crossing the mountain and spreading into the next valley. The second team is making a firebreak south of the fire to try to prevent it from going through one of these gaps and spreading." He looked back at the men and continued, "The Major and I think you're ready to put your training to work, so we have offered your help to the Forest Service. And I'm sure you're anxious to feel the heat and to smell the smoke firsthand—aren't you?"

The men laughed nervously.

"Right now there's a light wind blowing northeast to southwest," Silva continued turning back to the map. "We're going to put you on the east side of this western ridge and have you make a firebreak along the ridge. If the firebreak at the base of the mountain doesn't contain the fire in the valley than your firebreak will be the second line of defense to stop it or at least to give the two firefighting teams time to regroup and get up to your position." He tapped the ridge area on the map and continued. "As you can see from the map, this whole area has a lot of rocks and brush, but there aren't any trees on the ridge so your firebreak should be very effective and fairly easy to make. Lastly, your jump site." He paused and circled an area on the map with his finger, "I'd say that this area just below the ridge looks like a pretty good area. It's got a long slope, but isn't as steep as the surrounding area. Let's take a look when we do our first pass over it, then decide."

Silva set the wooden pointer down on the table and nodded to Wesley, who stood and to begin making assignments. "Captain, you're jumpmaster," he said looking at Tucker. "After you get everyone off the plane, come back and I want you to take over coordinating what the team's doing with the Forest Service firefighters."

"Yes, sir."

"Lieutenant," Wesley looked to Morris, "once you're on site, get the equipment issued as quickly as possible, then clear a three-foot-wide break about two hundred yards from the top of the ridge."

"Will do, sir."

"The Forest Service said that should stop the fire from crossing into the next valley. But I want one man posted on top of the ridge to watch firsthand what the valley fire's doing."

"Yes, sir."

"And if you see something from your vantage point that the Forest Service team needs to know, radio me or the captain, and we'll pass it on." Wesley turned to Silva. "Do you have anything else?"

"Yes, sorry I forgot about the walk out." Silva looked at Morris. "Once you've finished, the Forest Service will send a truck to pick you and all of your equipment up," he said, pointing to the map again, "here, where the ridge trail meets an old logging road. The trail down is getting overgrown, but they'll come up as far as they can to meet you. I've circled the road on your copy of the map." He looked around at the rest of the Triple Nickles. "And remember: don't leave anything behind. Parachutes, A-5's—all of the gear you take up there needs to come back. Good luck, men."

Wesley stood again and glanced at Boyle. "Sergeant, I want you to take two men and do a quick check of the A-5s we have packed and get them to the plane. We won't need any of the defusing gear, so don't bother with those packs. But take the ones with the extra shovels and Pulaski tools. And you'd better go ahead and make up another pack with extra canteens of water, it's supposed to get pretty hot out there today.

"Will do, sir."

Wesley looked at the group of men, "I told the pilot to be ready at 0830. You've got fifteen minutes to get your equipment together. You're dismissed. Let's move."

As the men stood, Boyle tapped Roger and Jackson on their shoulders and said loudly, "Come on lover boys. Follow me." Then he quietly added, "Y'all notice that the Captain ain't gonna get no calluses today. Them officers are thick as thieves."

Roger and Jackson followed Boyle shaking their heads.

CHAPTER FIFTEEN

Tucker sat in the copilot seat of the C-47 and looked out of the right window, watching Pendleton Field grow smaller as the plane climbed higher heading eastward into the clear blue, cloudless sky.

"Things down there sure look peaceful from up here, don't they?" He said almost to himself.

"They sure do. That's why I love flying," Jonesy answered with his hands firmly holding the control yoke and his eyes looking toward the horizon.

Tucker turned toward him. "You flew cargo trips between India and China before you came here, right?"

"Yup. I flew sixty-two missions over there." He paused and continued somberly. "Not many of us can say that."

Tucker thought about the comment. "Why's that?"

"Between the weather that changed in the blink of an eye and overloaded cargo, we lost a lot of planes and men flying over the Himalayas. Fifteen planes and a lot of men in one night alone while I was there."

"I guess you were pretty lucky then. What cargo were you flying?"

"You name it and we flew it into China. But the fifty-five-gallon drums of gasoline were the worse. Half the time we'd get caught in bad weather and the plane would start bouncing then the drums would break free and start rolling. One night I had a jeep and gas drums..." Jonesy stopped midsentence and pointed ahead of them. "Smoke. Better let Silva know we're almost there."

"Will do." Tucker got up and walked through the cockpit door and past the men sitting shoulder to shoulder chatting to each other in the long jump seat that ran from the front to the back of the plane. Their friendly conversations turned silent as he walked by.

He joined Silva at the open jump door.

"I just saw the smoke," Silva said to Tucker as the plane banked. "That's our target," he said pointing toward a mountain ridge high above the white smoke cloud that filled in the valley below. "Go tell Jonesy to make one more pass and we'll drop the wind streamers."

Tucker looked at him and smiled then picked up the newly installed hand-held microphone next to the jump door. "Jonesy, one more pass at altitude and we'll drop the streamers."

"Darn," Silva lamented, "old habits are hard to break."

Wind streamers, or wind drift indicators, were nineteen-foot-long pieces of colored crepe paper with a short metal rod at the end that told the jumpmaster wind speed and direction, and the correct release point for the paratroopers.

Tucker grabbed two red, weighted streamers from a box near the door, then laid down on the left side of the open door opposite Silva and awaited his signal. When it came he released both streamers watching as they gently fluttered to the ground.

"Wind is good. No gusts," Tucker said when he saw that the ribbons had landed in a clearing near the top of the ridge. "Looks like it's going to be a good day for jumping,"

"A great day," Silva agreed nodding to Tucker. He stood up from the doorway and picked the hand-held microphone off the hook "Jonesy, take her up. We'll drop the A-5s next pass."

"Yes, sir, up we go," a voice replied from the old speaker that Jimbo had also mounted next to the door. And a moment later the plane began its ascent.

Silva put the microphone back on the hook. "That sure makes life easier doesn't it? Especially when I remember it's there." He smiled as he patted Tucker on the back. "OK. Let's get ready."

Tucker turned to the men, and looked at Boyle "Get ready to hook up the A-5s."

Boyle nodded and pointed at Roger and Jackson to join him beside the canvas bags.

During the last two weeks of training, the procedures for checking the A-5's straps and parachute had become as routine as checking their own equipment. The three men knew what needed to be done and without talking moved around touching and tugging each of the canvas bags that held all of the gear they would need to fight fires and to survive in the forest for a couple of days, if need be. When they finished, they moved the bags close to the door and hooked their static lines to a metal rod that ran down the ceiling of the plane. When the bags were pushed out of the door their weight pulled the static line taunt and the parachute out of its deployment bag.

Tucker stood on the side of the open door watching the ground. "Approaching," he called, putting his right hand up. "Ready in three...two...one." He dropped his hand and Boyle, Roger, and Jackson pushed the first A-5 out. A moment later the parachute opened and its static line detached, hanging freely from the overhead rod. The other A-5s followed.

Silva watched the parachutes descend. When he was satisfied that they were going to land near the target area, he smiled at Tucker and gave him a thumbs up.

"Get ready," Tucker called to the seated men. "First nine men line up."

The men stood, and Tucker called. "Hook up."

They attached their static lined to the center rods.

"Check equipment."

They rechecked their chutes, straps and hooks.

"Stand in the door." The paratroopers moved forward and lined up in single file at the door, left foot forward waiting for the tap and the "Ready, go" command.

Jonesy's voice boomed over the speaker next to the door disrupting everyone's concentration.

"Captain, the major wants to talk to you."

Silva waved Tucker away. "Go talk to him. I can get everyone off the plane."

Tucker nodded and moved away from the open door. "Good luck, men. Let's show them what we can do!" He smiled at the men.

When Tucker came through the cockpit door, Jonesy nodded toward the headset resting on a hook near the co-pilot's seat. Tucker again maneuvered his tall frame into the tight, thinly padded metal seat, put the headset on and took the handheld microphone off of the hook by his window.

"Tower One, this is Captain Freeman."

The line was filled with static.

Jonesy looked at the dial on the radio box under his left-side window, and turned it back and forth. The static continued.

"Cap...a...bal...tur..." Major Wesley's words were cut off by the loud static.

Jonesy turned the dial on his radio box again then motioned Tucker to check his microphone connection.

Tucker wiggled it, but the static continued. He shrugged at Jonesy, who looked up at the overhead radio control panel with furrowed eyebrows.

"I'm sorry, sir. We're having trouble with our radio," Tucker said raising his voice. "Please repeat."

Jonesy checked his headset connections. The static continued. He took his microphone off the hook next to his seat, pulled the plug out of the box below it, pushed it back in and gave it a twist. The static stopped. He smiled broadly at Tucker then turned the radio dial from headset to speaker just as Silva appeared in the cockpit doorway.

"Everyone's down," he said quietly, "safe and sound."

Tucker gave him a thumbs up, then clicked his microphone on again. "Tower One. This is Bravo. The men are on the ground, and it looks like our radio is working."

"Great," Wesley's static voice said over the speaker. "But the mission has changed a bit. A Forest Service plane saw what they think is a Japanese balloon in the valley west of the fire. Sounds like it may be down the other side of the ridge from where you're making the firebreak. The Colonel wants you to take a team..."

Wesley's voice stopped mid-sentence and the men in the cockpit heard a series of clicks. Thinking it was their radio again, Jonesy reached for the radio dial just as Richardson's voice boomed from the speaker, loud and clear. "...And get that goddamn balloon and those bombs. I need to show Headquarters you're doing something for this war besides sitting on your thumbs."

Tucker looked at Silva questioningly. Silva shrugged then asked loud enough to be heard over the radio, "What about the firebreak?"

Richardson's answer came back to Tucker not Silva. "Captain, your priority is the balloon not the fire. Do you hear me?"

"Yes, sir."

Silva leaned to the microphone. "We told the Forest Service we'd make the firebreak they needed. If that fire spreads…"

Richardson broke in. "Silva, we work for the army, not the Forest Service. May I remind you that you're a guest at my base and on that plane."

Silva opened his mouth to reply, but Tucker put his finger to his lips and shook his head at Silva. Silva closed his mouth and took a deep breath. Tucker was right. They would talk after the radio was off.

Richardson continued, "Captain, you have your orders—get that balloon. Major Wesley will have the coordinates for you by the time you're on the ground. Over and out."

Tucker put the headset and microphone on their hooks then turned to Silva, who was still furious.

"That stupid son-of-a-bitch," Silva shouted to no one in particular. "Why can't we finish the firebreak then get the balloon. It's not going anywhere."

Tucker put his hand up, motioning Silva to stop. "He told me to get the balloon, not how many men I needed to take to do the job." He smiled at Silva. "I'll take five men with me, and Morris and the rest of the men can work on the firebreak."

Tucker climbed out of the co-pilot seat, and nodded to Jonesy. "Looks like I'm jumping today. Just give me a couple of minutes to get my parachute on!"

"Take your time, I'll circle until you're ready."

CHAPTER SIXTEEN

Floating downward on a gentle breeze, Tucker looked at the valley below him. The smoke filled every contour, crag and chasm of the valley floor making the surrounding mountain ranges look like they were islands sitting in a lake of gray water.

Tucker gave the left shroud lines a slight tug maneuvering toward the jump site and then looked back at the valley. *It's hard to believe that a fire is raging under that cloud of smoke*, he thought as he made one more adjustment. A moment later he made a perfect landing on Catwalk Peak.

By the time he took off his harness and rolled up his chute, he saw that the men had already opened and unpacked the A-5s with the Forest Service tools. A dozen men had already taken off their shirts and in a synchronized motion like an undulating wave from the beginning of the line to the end, they cleared a swath of small plants and brush with their Pulaski tools while they laughed and chatted.

Willie was talking on the radio with Angel on his shoulder when Tucker walked by. “Welcome, Captain. The major says that he’ll have those coordinates in the next five minutes. And the lieutenant is up on the ridge,” he said motioning with his head.

“Sounds good.” Tucker set his parachute down and picked up a pair of binoculars from one of the A-5s. He walked up the ridge to a large flat rock where Morris was scanning the horizon with his binoculars.

“Wesley radioed with the news about the balloon,” Morris said from behind the binoculars. “But I thought we’d go ahead and work on the firebreak until you got here. It looks like the fire is moving south-southwest.

Tucker pulled a small map from his breast pocket and spread it out on the rock. He traced the area with his finger. “That’s the area where the firefighters are now.

Morris continued scanning. "There's smoke in a gap south of us," Morris said as he continued to scan the valley and mountainside with his binoculars. "But I can't tell if there's any fire there or if it's just drifting smoke."

Tucker studied the map, "I see the gap. Hopefully, it's just drifting smoke," he said as his finger followed the contour of the gap on the map. "But watch it closely. It connects to the valley behind us. I don't want you to be caught up here with fire on both sides of the mountain."

Morris lowered the field glasses letting the leather strap around his neck catch and hold them on his chest. He looked at Tucker questioningly. "I thought we *all* were supposed to go to retrieve the balloon."

"Richardson didn't say *all.* I think six of us can handle it. The rest of you need to cover our backs and make sure the fire doesn't jump this ridge."

Willie appeared on the path, talking into the portable field radio. "Here's Captain Freeman, sir," he said as he held the radio out for Tucker. "It's Major Wesley. He has the coordinates for the balloon."

Tucker cradled the radio in his shoulder as he took a paper and pencil from his shirt pocket. "Ready, sir."

"Latitude 45 degrees, 51 minutes, 39 seconds north. Longitude 117 degrees, 57 minutes, 29 seconds west."

Tucker repeated the numbers as he wrote the coordinates on the paper.

"Got it, Major. We're on our way."

"Good Luck, Captain. Out."

Tucker handed the radio back to Willie. "Thank you, Willie."

Morris looked at the coordinates that Tucker had written down then at the map. "Looks like the balloon is in the western valley a couple miles north of the gap that's filling with smoke."

"If the wind keeps blowing northeast to southwest we should be fine. And hopefully the Forest Service will contain the fire long before it hits the gap."

Morris walked up to the top of the ridge and looked down the mountainside the men would have to traverse to get to the valley. "You're going to have to go down some pretty steep terrain to get there."

Tucker joined him on the ridge and looked down the mountainside. "Whew-y. That's an understatement." He picked up the map, folded it and put it in his pocket. "Guess I'd better get started." Tucker headed off the ridge toward the rest of the men with Morris and Willie following.

"Men," Tucker called out, "gather round and take a knee."

The men put their tools down and made their way to Tucker.

"I just received the coordinates for a balloon that was sited. It's on the other side of this ridge, down some pretty rough terrain." Tucker paused and looked at the men in front of him. "Jackson, Roger, Dixie, Willie and Sawyer, you're with me. The rest of you will stay here with the Lieutenant and continue working on the firebreak."

Morris nodded to Tucker then turned to the men who were staying behind. "Let's get moving. We've got a lot of work to do." Following Morris, the eleven men walked back to the tools they'd laid down, regrouped and started working on the firebreak again.

Tucker looked at the five men that were going with him. "Willie, bring one radio for us, and make sure the second one is set up for the lieutenant."

"Will do, sir," Willie answered then added. "And, of course, Angel will be coming too."

Tucker looked at the bobbing pigeon on Willie's shoulder and realized that her presence with them was so normal he never even noticed her anymore. "Of course, she's coming with us." He reached out and stroked Angel's head. "If the radio doesn't work in the valley, she's our back-up."

She cooed.

Roger stood up. "Sir, do you remember that we didn't bring the A-5 with the defusing equipment when we left. How are we supposed to get the bombs defused?"

Tucker closed his eyes and shook his head. "Shit."

Jackson rose and looked around. "Jimbo always carries his tools. They'll work." He turned and scanned the men on the fire line. "Hey Jimbo, we need to borrow your tools to take with us in case we need to defuse any bombs."

Jimbo looked at Jackson and groaned, but after a moment he undid his waist pack of tools and walked over and handed them to him. "These was my daddy's, and I'm holding you personally responsible. You better bring them all back!"

Tucker stepped forward and patted Jimbo on the back, "Thank you, Jimbo. We'll bring them back. I promise." He turned back to the others while Jackson re-adjusted the tool belt for his waist. "Roger, make sure everyone has at least one canteen."

Roger nodded.

"Dixie, bring your let-down rope, just in case we need rope for something."

"Got it right here with my gear." He unhooked it from his parachute harness and slung it over his shoulder.

"And Sawyer, how about bringing a first-aid kit."

"Will do, sir," he replied as dug through one of the A-5s until he came up with a small backpack marked with a red cross in a white circle.

When everyone was ready, Tucker led them to the top of the ridge.

"Guess we know who the Captain's favorite boys are," Boyle said as he appeared next to Jimbo. "And ain't they the lucky ones. Yup, they won't be sweating on no chain gang today."

Jimbo twisted his head around and gave Boyle a hard look before turning back to watch Jackson disappear with his tools. Once he was out of sight, Jimbo pushed past Boyle without saying a word and joined the others clearing brush.

CHAPTER SEVENTEEN

Tucker walked back and forth looking at his map and scanning the landscape while Sawyer, Dixie, Willie, Roger, and Jackson sat on a large, flat granite rock watching.

Ten minutes later he stopped and smiled. He found what he'd been looking for—a trail—and waved the men over.

Before Tucker had parachuted earlier, Silva had given him a fifteen-minute tutorial on what he and the men needed to do to safely hike down the steep six-thousand-foot mountain. He'd explained how Rocky Mountain elk and bighorn sheep routinely moved between the mountain ridges covered with native bunchgrass and the valley's year-round streams. The path they made would the easiest and safest way to get to the valley floor—they knew what they were doing, even if the well-worn trails were narrow and had a lot of switchbacks. Silva also gave Tucker his topography map and marked a couple of areas where he'd likely find the trailhead to the valley.

"Are you sure this is the way down?" Sawyer asked staring down the steep, rocky slope.

"Doctor Silva said it might be hard to see at first, but I'm pretty sure that's an animal trail. It looks flat and well-worn like he described."

The men strained to see what Tucker was talking about.

"And, he did say that it would be very narrow up here," Tucker added.

Dixie shook his head. "Sure doesn't look like much to me."

"I'll take the lead. Hold on to the boulders and outcrops to steady yourselves. We'll take it slow and easy," Tucker said as looked down the treacherously steep, rocky incline.

The men fell in a tight line behind him.

After a half-hour of struggling down the narrow path between outcrops of granite and huge boulders, the terrain changed abruptly—the path widened from six inches to a foot or more, scrub brush and grasses had taken root in the nooks and crannies of every large rock, and the vertical drop next to the trail became sheer in many spots.

"Captain, do you think we got off the trail?" Dixie asked as he grabbed a branch of brush to stop himself from sliding sideways.

"Not according to the map Silva marked for us. He predicted that this is the route they would follow," Tucker answered as he grabbed a second scrub brush branch to stop himself from sliding. "And, we're still following the flattest area I see."

"I'm happy I'm not a mountain goat," Willie said looking down the steep drop off over his left shoulder, "I don't know how they do it. This is making my stomach sick."

"Don't look down, Willie!" Roger shouted from behind him. "They can do it because they always look straight ahead. They know if they look downhill they'd likely fall!"

Willie quickly turned his head back to face the path. A second later his left foot slipped downhill and he shrieked as he grabbed an uphill branch of scrub brush.

"What'd I tell you," Roger teased.

"Roger, what's wrong with you?" Willie squealed. Angel began moving around in her shoulder harness. "You're making me and Angel nervous."

Jackson listened to their exchange as he followed closely behind Roger, grabbing branches to hang on to as soon as Roger released them. "Yeah Rog, you're making me nervous, too. And why you always pickin' on Will..." The small branch Jackson was holding snapped. He desperately grabbed for another branch but lost his balance and started sliding downhill off the trail. He twirled his arms backwards trying to find his balance, but continued to slide on the loose gravelly rocks. A scrub brush finally stopped his feet but his momentum pitched his torso forward and he began somersaulting down the mountainside.

Without thinking, Roger instinctively let go of the branch he was holding to try and help Jackson. And a moment later he was sliding down the mountainside as if he was sitting on an invisible Flexible Flyer sled, following the tumbling Jackson.

When Dixie moved to take off his backpack, Tucker's arm shot out across his chest to hold him back. "Don't do anything stupid, or you'll be with them!" Tucker said using his arm to push Dixie against the uphill rock. As soon as he felt Dixie's resistance stop, Tucker removed his arm and looked past him to Willie and Sawyer. "Don't worry, we'll get them. Smartly."

A thicket of brush finally stopped Roger's fall two hundred feet below the path. He sat there for a moment to catch his breath and to see how he was. When he was sure he was OK he scooted to a large boulder in the middle of the brush, leaned against it, and waved to let Tucker know he was OK. Then he turned his head to peek around the rock to see if he could spot Jackson. He gasped loudly. Jackson was lying below him on the edge of a small flat rock that overhung a sheer drop.

"Jackson's about a hundred feet below me on the edge of a cliff," Roger yelled up to Tucker. "He's moaning, but he ain't moving."

"Yeah, I see him. We'll be down to help you both. Stay where you are. And don't think about trying to help Jackson by yourself," Tucker called back.

Tucker turned to the three men next to him. "First, let's sit down real nice and easy on this path then we can talk about how we're going to help the men and get back on the trail." Without a word, the men pressed their backs into the uphill mountainside and slowly bent their knees then walked their feet out until they were sitting on the path.

"OK," Tucker continued when the men were settled next to him. "I don't think we can make it back up here, but I might see a switchback," he said pointing downhill. "About two hundred feet to the right and below where Roger's sitting."

"I think I see it," Sawyer said pointing to a smooth a flat line in the distant rocky terrain. "Yeah, that does look like a trail."

Willie and Dixie followed Sawyer's gaze and nodded in agreement.

"We'll head over there once we get Roger and Jackson. But first let's figure out what we need to do to get them."

"Can we rope down?" Dixie asked.

Tucker looked around. "There's nothing around here to tie it to, and we'd be short of where they are anyway."

"They slid," Willie offered. "If we know we're going to, maybe we can do a better job."

"That's probably our only choice." Tucker shook his head agreeing. "And once we get to Roger, I want the three of you to move to the flat area by the lower trail while I go down and get Jackson."

"He's at the edge of a cliff," Sawyer said. "Don't you want some help?"

"Thanks, but it looks like there's barely enough room for two people near the ledge, less enough three," Tucker answered.

Tucker scooted closer to the edge of the trail where they were sitting. "OK men, let's see if we can slide down to Roger, but with more control than he did. Dig your heels in if you start going too fast, and don't use your hands to try to stop yourself, you'll just tear them up." Tucker pushed off, bent his knees slightly, and started sliding toward Roger.

Sawyer eased to the edge and followed.

Dixie turned to Willie before he pushed off. "You be careful with our girl, Willie."

"That goes without saying." Willie said as he turned and gave Angel a little kiss through the webbing of her shoulder harness.

Dixie saluted Willie and went over the side, sliding and bouncing down the hill.

Willie scooted to the edge and watched as the others neared Roger. He turned to Angel again. "Sorry, but it looks like we're in for a bumpy ride." He slid off the edge with Angel softly cooing on his shoulder.

Tucker dug his heels in the hard, rocky ground when he was just above Roger's position, but slid ten feet beyond him before he could get stopped. He turned over and slowly belly-crawled up hill.

Sawyer was the first one to make it to Roger, and was already unpacking his first-aid kit when Dixie and Willie slid in beside them.

"You OK?" Tucker asked Roger when he made it back up the hill and joined the group.

"Yeah, just some scrapes and scratches." Roger answered. "But I'm not sure about Jackson. He's been moaning a lot. I keep looking, but he still ain't moved."

Dixie stretched his neck to look. "Holy shit. He's lucky he ain't moving. He's about a foot from going over the edge."

Tucker looked at the precarious perch that Jackson was lying on and shook his head. "You all work your way over to the path down there, and I'll go get Jackson."

Sawyer grabbed Tucker's arm. "I'll go." Sawyer slung the first-aid backpack over his shoulder. "I'm the medic, you're the leader." And before Tucker could say anything, Sawyer moved and began sliding down the hill his feet displacing small rocks that rolled ahead of him pelting Jackson.

Jackson moaned and began to stir.

"Don't move." Sawyer yelled, "I'm almost there. Just please don't move yet." He dug his feet in harder to slow his descent and minimize the rocks he was showering on Jackson. It worked.

As he slowed and got closer, Sawyer scooted left to a scrub brush five feet above Jackson's head. He tested the shrub's largest branch while hanging onto another one to make sure the brush and the branch were going to hold him. Convinced they would, he looked down toward Jackson and did a quick assessment.

His heart sank when he saw blood spreading on the rock under Jackson's head.

"Jackson, can you hear me? If you can, I'm here to help you. But please don't move."

Jackson raised his head slightly and Sawyer noticed a small gash on his forehead pumping blood. "Damn if heads cuts don't always try to bleed you out," he said to himself, relieved that that was the cause of all the blood.

Jackson tried to raise himself to his elbow. He groaned with pain and put his head back down.

"I told you not to move," Sawyer screamed. "You're on the edge of a cliff, you idiot."

Jackson turned his head and looked. "Oh shit. I'm gonna be sick."

"No you're not. You'll be fine once I get you off that ledge. Just don't move until I tell you." Sawyer turned over onto his stomach, his head downhill. He tugged at the branch he was holding in his left hand again. It held. He reached out with his right hand, but couldn't maneuver close enough to reach Jackson.

"Jackson, listen to me. I can't get any closer. I need you to give me your hand."

Jackson slowly brought his arm forward. It was a couple of inches away from Sawyer.

"You need to scoot up just a little more."

"I don't know if I can move."

"You have to. Slide your right knee up, then use it to push yourself forward. Just a couple more inches and I can reach you."

Slowly, Jackson did as he was told wincing with every move he made.

"OK. I got your hand. One more push," Sawyer ordered. When Jackson pushed, Sawyer grabbed his wrist. "Now you grab ahold of my wrist and hang on."

Jackson held onto Sawyer's wrist for a moment, then loosened his grip. "Man, I'm hurting,"

"You're gonna be really hurting if you slide backwards," Sawyer shot back. "Don't you think about letting go of me. I ain't got no leverage to pull you uphill. We need to do this together."

"OK."

"Now I'm gonna scoot backwards and pull you along as much as I can, but it would really help if you could push yourself toward me at the same time. Ready?"

Jackson tightened his grip again and used his knee to push himself up a couple of more inches. Sawyer continued to back up bringing Jackson with him a few inches at a time.

When they'd made it about thirty feet, Sawyer stopped, exhausted. "I need to rest for a couple of minutes." He relaxed his grip but still held on. Jackson did the same.

"You doing OK?" Sawyer asked though the pain that was beginning to scream in his own arm.

"Yeah."

"Would you do me a favor before we get moving again?"

"Yeah." Jackson replied, his head lying on the rock.

"Use your free hand to take your front pack off. You'll be able to crawl easier without it."

Jackson lifted his head and looked at him incredulously through pain filled eyes. "Are you crazy? That's Jimbo's tools. I lose them, I might as well jump off a cliff."

Sawyer shook his head. "OK, let's go."

They kept moving with push and pulls until they made it to the flat area close to the other men, then Dixie and Willie rushed forward to help Sawyer.

They picked Jackson up under his arms and half carried him, half dragged him to an area they had cleared of rocks, then gently laid him down while Dixie propped his head on a backpack.

"Sometimes you're more trouble than you're worth Lonnie Jackson," Dixie scolded. "And if it weren't for

Billie, we likely would've left your black ass hanging over that cliff."

Willie grimaced and whacked Dixie's head lightly. "You know you don't mean that, Dixie Flynn."

"Yes, I do."

"Thanks, Dixie, you're a real friend," Jackson replied with a painful smile.

Sawyer sat down next to Jackson and pulled bandages, cotton gauze and a tube of cream from the first-aid kit. He wet the gauze with water from his canteen.

Tucker joined the group. "Good work, Sawyer. Thank you."

Sawyer nodded, "My pleasure, sir."

Tucker turned and leaned toward Jackson checking his arms and legs while Sawyer cleaned the blood off of Jackson's face and head with the gauze.

"He's got a lot of small cuts and scrapes, but nothing appears to be broken," Tucker said quietly to Sawyer. Then he bent closer to Jackson. "You are one lucky man."

"Yup, that's me, real lucky," Jackson answered with his eyes closed.

When Sawyer finished cleaning the gash on Jackson's head he pulled it together with a small piece of adhesive tape, put cream over the area, and topped it with a square bandage.

"You may need a couple of stitches, but this'll hold it together and stop the bleeding for now."

Jackson moaned and opened his eyes. "Thanks, Sawyer. I'm already feeling better, just real achy everywhere."

Sawyer picked up a morphine syrette from his first-aid kit, lifted Jackson's shirt to expose his belly and injected the morphine under Jackson's skin.

"That should take care of the pain," he said putting the used syrette in a small bag.

"You'll feel a lot better in a minute," Tucker said patting Jackson's shoulder.

"That was some shortcut you and Roger found," Dixie chuckled to Jackson, "but it probably saved us a lot of time."

Jackson grimaced as he slowly sat up and touched his head. "Ouch!"

Roger knelt next to Jackson. "You really OK?"

"Heck yeah. Guess this proves my head's harder than yours!"

"Well, it appears that the morphine is working," Tucker said to Jackson with a smile. "You and Roger rest a couple more minutes, then let's see if we can walk down the last three thousand feet instead of rolling!"

Roger and Dixie helped Jackson stand, while everyone else picked up their gear. Tucker grabbed the first aid kit backpack from Sawyer. "My turn to carry it. Give your back and arm a rest."

Sawyer smiled and nodded.

When the weary men finally descended the last hundred feet of the eastern mountain slope they were met by a lush narrow valley with a shallow rocky river that gently meandered between two steep pine treed slopes. And the faint smell of smoke.

"Willie, get on the radio and let Morris know we're in the valley—and that we can smell smoke," Tucker said. "Ask if he has an update on the fire."

"Will do, sir." Willie carefully removed Angel from the shoulder harness and set her down on the ground. She cooed and pecked at the ground, then took off for a short flight while Willie got the radio out of his backpack and turned it on.

Dixie stood on the balls of his feet and rocked back to his heels. "My legs are screaming. They've forgotten what flat ground feels like."

"It is nice, isn't it?" Tucker said as he bent down and spread his map out. The other men gathered behind him and looked over his shoulders.

"We're right about here," he said as he pointed to a spot on the map. "The balloon should be in this area, a mile or two north of us."

Willie appeared in front of Tucker. "Captain, I talked to Lieutenant Morris. He said that a secondary fire started in that gap south of us, so we need to watch our backs."

"Great," Tucker said sarcastically. "We sure as hell don't want to be caught in this narrow valley in a fire." He stood and quickly folded the map. "Let's get moving and find that balloon."

Willie stepped forward. "He also told me to tell you that once we have the balloon we need to keep heading north along the river. The Forest Service has all of their men working the fire, so they left a truck for us on an old fire road and said we need to head west—fast—once we get there."

Tucker put the map in his pocket. "OK, let's move."

As the men picked up their gear, Tucker moved next to Sawyer and whispered. "Stay close to Jackson, OK?"

"Will do, sir," Sawyer replied softly, "but how about you getting him to let go of Jimbo's tool belt. That would lighten him up."

Tucker nodded and walked to where Jackson was quietly standing. "I'm going to carry this," Tucker said as he swiftly undid the tool pack belt and put it on himself.

Tucker's quick movement took Jackson by surprise. "Just remember it's me he's going to kill if anything happens to them."

"I'll take full responsibility," Tucker said as he patted Jackson reassuringly on the back.

Jackson winced with pain.

The men spread out and walked along the eastern side of the river through tall grasses, over rocks, around brush, but always staying near the river where they had the best view of both sides.

Tucker kept looking over his shoulder as he walked, watching the gray wisps of smoke getting thicker behind them. He open this mouth to tell the others when Willie's voice erased the thought.

"The balloon! I see it!"

Everyone rushed forward to look at their first Japanese Fu-Go balloon spread out on the ground like a huge white tarp on the other side of the river.

Without a word, they all ran through the water toward the balloon, not noticing that the breeze from south had picked up a little and that tendrils of smoke were snaking through the trees on the steep slopes just behind them.

Everyone gathered around the gondola surveying the components—armament, fuses, control switches—

they were looking at and comparing them in their minds to what they had worked with in class. And thinking about what they needed to do to disarm the three incendiary bombs attached to the gondola.

"A fuse box and incendiary bombs," Sawyer offered. "Same as the thermite bomb mock-ups we did in class, just a different color, right?"

"I think so. What do you say, Captain?" Roger asked.

When Tucker didn't answer, the men looked around and noticed he wasn't with the group huddled around the gondola. He had left and was walking around the seventy-foot paper balloon, staring at a small fire that had just started in dried grass fifty feet away.

He suddenly turned back to the men and yelled, "Sawyer, Roger…you're defusing. Dixie and Willie…with me.

"What you want me to do, sir?" Jackson asked.

"You hand Sawyer and Roger whatever tools they need." He took off Jimbo's tool belt and handed it to him. "And make sure you get them all back," he added with a smile.

He turned to Dixie and Willie and pointed to the small fire. "Dixie, let's see if we can put that out before it spreads."

"Got it," Dixie said as he ran toward the fire.

"Willie, start cutting the balloon shrouds. Dixie and I will be right back to help get it away from the gondola—and the bombs."

Willie unsheathed his army knife and frantically began cutting the three-strand manila rope shrouds that connected the balloon to the gondola while Tucker and Dixie stomped the nearby fire out.

When the last shrouds were cut, the three men grabbed the lines still connected to the balloon and began dragging it away from the gondola toward the river as smoke drifted over them and small cinders began to sparkle in the air. Before they made it to the river a cinder floated down and landed on the paper orb igniting it in a fiery blaze.

At the gondola, Jackson dropped the tools he was holding on the ground next to Sawyer. He jumped up and began trying to stomp out pockets of fire that were closing in on the gondola.

Tucker saw Jackson and dropped the shrouds he was holding and motioned for Dixie and Willie to stop. "Forget the balloon. We need to help Jackson. The fire's closing in on the gondola."

They dropped the balloon shrouds and ran toward the gondola, stomping flames as they raced against the quickly spreading fire.

A few moments later Tucker realized that their effort to help Jackson stomp out the fire was useless. The fire was winning.

"Head for the river," he yelled above the increasing roar of the fire. I'll get Roger and Sawyer."

Willie put two fingers to his lips and whistled for Angel, who came before his whistle finished. He quickly shoved her into his shirt, then helped Dixie almost drag an exhausted and hurting Jackson into the water.

At the gondola, Sawyer and Roger were huddled over an incendiary bomb, cautiously undoing a wooden screw from the side of the steel tube that gave them access to the creep spring, safety pin and arming wire inside the 5-kilogram incendiary bomb. Once inside, it only took seconds to safely defuse it and dump the black powder and thermite filling.

Roger smiled at Sawyer when he had finished, then carefully reached for the last live bomb that was hanging from the metal ring around the gondola.

Tucker rushed up and stopped his hand before Roger touched it. “Leave it! We’ve got to get out of here.”

Sawyer looked at him, bewildered. “But we just have one more to defuse.”

“Forget it. That’s an order. We’ve gotta get to the river. Now!”

Roger and Sawyer looked around, and for the first time since they’d begun defusing the bombs they noticed the fire that was intensifying around them.

“Holy shit,” they yelled in unison as they jumped up and ran toward the river following Tucker’s lead.

Sawyer suddenly stopped, turned around and ran back. He picked up Jimbo’s tools and put them in his backpack. Then he noticed the two bombs they’d defused on the ground and dropped them in the pack. He put the pack on as he ran for his life toward the river again.

The heat from the encroaching fire triggered the last live bomb on the gondola to explode sending a hail-stone of metal and fire shot out in every direction just as Sawyer stepped into the river.

The sound of the blast made the others stop to see what happened. They turned around just in time to see Sawyer knocked down by a piece of flying debris.

Tucker immediately threw his backpack to Dixie then ran back toward the blazing fire to get Sawyer.

CHAPTER EIGHTEEN

Dirty, sweaty, battered, and tired, Tucker's team got out of the Forest Service truck in front of their barracks and were getting their gear when the screen door quickly opened and the rest of the Triple Nickles rushed toward them.

"What happened?" Morris asked, looking at Tucker as he took his backpack from him.

"It's a long story. Let me get cleaned up and I'll tell you all about it."

Jimbo bent down to pick up one of the backpack stacked on the ground when he noticed Jackson's bandaged head. He stood up to take a closer look.

"I found a shortcut down the mountain," Jackson offered.

"Oh," Jimbo said as he looked around. "And where's Sawyer at?"

"He's in the hospital," Roger chimed in. "The fire set off one of the bombs and Sawyer got thrown by the explosion. He hit his head pretty hard and his arm got burned."

"The doctor thinks he's going to be fine," Tucker added. "He just wanted to keep an eye on him for a day or two."

Jackson walked up to Jimbo with his head hanging low. "Jimbo, I'm real sorry, but your tools got left when we ran from the fire."

Jimbo stared at Jackson with a somber face for a few seconds, then he finally said, "I'm just happy y'all are OK." He put his arm around Jackson and helped him into the barracks.

Inside, Roger sat down on the edge of his bunk and rubbed his neck. "Man, I got muscles aching I didn't even know I had."

Boyle walked over and patted him on the back. "Just wait until tomorrow. You're gonna find more new ones!"

The screen door swung open and Major Wesley stepped in.

"Atten-hut," Boyle barked as he stood.

"As you were, men," Wesley said stopping the men as they began to rise. "I just came by to tell you that John McNally, the regional head of the Forest Service sends his thanks. He said your firebreak was a lifesaver. Without it his men wouldn't have been able to contain the second canyon fire."

Wesley looked around until he saw Tucker. He stepped toward him and said sincerely, "Captain, I'm sorry that you couldn't get the gondola or the bombs, but I'm happy you and your men are OK." He smiled, and continued. "Of course, Richardson exploded when he found out you left men on the ridge. But, you made the right decision. More men in the valley wouldn't have changed the outcome."

"Thank you, sir."

"Now, I want you and your men to take tomorrow off to rest. You've earned it." Wesley turned and headed for the door. "Hangar A, 0800 on Friday."

"Yes, sir," Tucker said.

When Wesley left, Jackson stood up in front of Tucker. "Captain, I want to thank you...and Sawyer, for saving my ass on that mountain."

Roger stood up next to Jackson. "Yeah, and my ass too. And I guess I need to thank you for ordering us to get away from that gondola when you did. If we would've stayed, we'd all be in the hospital."

"Or worse," Dixie added.

"I'm just sorry we didn't bring back the bombs," Roger said with dismay.

"You men did your best." Tucker said with a smile. "That's all I'll ever ask."

The screen door to the barracks opened again. This time it was Terrance carrying a large jug of coffee, cups, and a whole tray of sandwiches.

"I figured there weren't no reason for y'all walking all the way over to the mess hall," Terrance said. He set the coffee and sandwiches down, then got two crackers out of his pocket and handed them to Willie. "And something for our little Angel, too."

Terrance poured the hot, black coffee. Then he stepped back and watched the men grab sandwiches and their coffees, and smiled. "Y'all rest good tonight cause tomorrow night we're invited to join the service unit at Betty's. First rounds on the house—if we can get Dixie to play."

Dixie smile. "You know I will. Even if Betty don't give out a free beer."

Roger stood up next to Dixie, and asked teasingly. "That's mighty generous of you, but what about the rest of us? I know I'd sure appreciate a free beer."

The rest of the men hooted at Dixie.

"Now I didn't say I was gonna turn down the offer. You'll get your free one, don't worry."

The men cheered.

Roger patted him on his back. "He's our man, right?"

Everyone cheered again as Dixie walked toward Tucker.

"Captain, I hope you'll join us," Dixie said.

"Sure. Thanks, I'd like that." *At last*, he thought and smiled.

Dixie nodded and headed toward the showers.

Boyle bumped him as he walked by. “He ain’t one of us,” Boyle whispered loudly, “and not all of us want him there.”

Dixie pushed past Boyle and saw Tucker looking at him. It was obvious that he’d overheard Boyle.

CHAPTER NINETEEN

Jimbo pulled the bus to a stop in front of Betty's Bar and the men pushed forward as soon as he opened the bus door. Dixie and his saxophone were allowed to go first, but the other Triple Nickles and service unit men followed on his heels.

"Terrance," Jimbo called from the bus, "if they're taking orders, tell Sadie I want the usual—a cola and a big steak. I'll be in as soon as I park the bus."

"Will do," Terrance answered as the bus doors closed. When he turned toward the front door of the bar he saw Morris driving down the street in *Lucille* with the top down. Morris stopped in front of Betty's to give Jimbo time to backup and turn around in the road before he tried to maneuver the bus into the narrow alley next to the bar.

"You sure you won't have just one beer with us, Lieutenant?" Terrance called as he made his way to the front door.

"Thanks, Terrance, but not tonight," he answered. "Pearl is fixing me dinner at Miss Rae's."

"OK. Well, see you tomorrow then. Excuse me but I need to get inside."

Jimbo walked around the corner and waved to Morris as he drove off, then turned to Terrance. "No need to hurry Terrance, ain't no one gonna steal Big Betty. She's all yours."

Terrance grinned sheepishly as he opened the bar door.

"Course if I was a drinking man," Jimbo continued as he followed Terrance into the bar, "she might not look so bad."

The dark, smoke-filled bar was packed with fifty men in uniform, seven women customers, and Sadie and Mable hustling trays of drinks between the tables as the din of chatter grew louder and raunchier.

Jimbo joined Willie, Jackson and Billie, and Roger and Lulu at a table near the stage. They were intently listening to Dixie play his sax while one of the service unit men accompanied him on the piano, and a large, buxom woman wearing a midnight black sequenced dress belted out the blues.

The rest of the Triple Nickles and the dozen service unit men that had just arrived pushed small tables together to make one long table next to Boyle and the other service unit men who had come to the bar earlier.

Boyle's table was already lined with empty beer bottles and the men sitting with him were becoming more rowdy with every round.

"How about another round," Boyle called to Sadie.

"How about you eating some food instead of drinking more," Sadie yelled back as she picked up empties and put them on a tray.

"You gonna get us more beer or not?"

"Not," she said in a huff as she picked up the tray and walked away.

"You ain't getting no tip tonight, Sadie!" Boyle yelled after her. He slid his chair back and told the others that he'd get more beer himself.

Terrance sat at the bar sipping a bottle of Coca-Cola and talking to Betty. "Baby, you know I'd love to stay, but I got to get up early and cook." He leaned closer. "How about I stay over Saturday night?"

"And you knows that I got to get up early and go to church on Sunday." Betty picked up a wet rag and sauntered down the bar wiping it. "How come you always got more excuses than time for me?" She asked as she put her hands on her broad hips.

"Awww. Baby, you're killing me. Believe me, I want to stay tonight. But I can't."

"Um-hummm." She began wiping the counter again as she rolled her eyes.

"I'm sure we can..." Terrance was stopped in mid-sentence when Boyle stumbled into him.

"Another round of drinks for my friends," Boyle stuttered as he fumbled to get money out of his pocket.

"I think you, and your friends, already had enough tonight," Betty said sternly crossing her arms across her chest.

Boyle threw the wad of money that he fished out of his pocket on the bar, and turned to Terrance. "How about you tell your girlfriend to get us a drink. She can't seem to hear me."

Terrance got off the bar stool, picked up the money, and put it back in Boyle's shirt pocket. "I think Betty's right. Y'all already had enough to drink."

Boyle pushed Terrance out of his way and stumbled back to his table.

"Betty ain't serving us no more," he announced loudly. "I'm tired of being told I can't do this, I can't do that. Tired of it. Let's go somewhere else."

Terrance stepped in front of Boyle. "Sarge, there's no place else to go," he said softly. "How about Jimbo and I take you home."

Boyle pushed him out of the way and looked around at the service unit men he'd been drinking with for the last hour and smirked. "I bet we can get a drink at the Twilight."

Jimbo quickly appeared next to Boyle. "Sarge, you know you can't go there."

Boyle took the money out of his pocket, walked around Jimbo, and fanned the money at the service unit men. "I say we can go there or anywhere else we want."

He looked at his drinking companions. "First round's on me." The dozen men stood from the table and followed Boyle to the front door.

Terrance rushed past Jimbo and headed for the side door near the kitchen. "Slow them down. I'll get some help."

Jimbo nodded to Terrance and quickly blocked the front door. He crossed his arms and puffed up his chest, which made him look three times the size of any of the other men.

Boyle's face filled with rage. "Get out the way, Nigger. That's an order."

"Sorry, Sarge, I can't." Jimbo answered as he held his ground.

Boyle looked around, and then remembered the side door. "Come on," he called to his followers as he headed to the other door.

Roger and Jackson jumped up from their table and rushed to the side door to try to block it, but were easily pushed out of the way by the irate, drunken men.

Jimbo opened the front door and tried to stop Boyle and his drunken friends when they came around the outside corner, but the men spread out and easily side-stepped him.

Led by Boyle, the men stumbled down the middle of the street, heading for the railroad crossing.

On the other side of the tracks, two men wearing jeans, cowboy hats and boots were leaning with their backs against a pickup truck watching the scene that was unfolding outside Betty's Bar.

Arlo, the taller of the two men, stood up a little straighter when he saw the drunks getting close to the invisible boundary—the railroad track—that everyone knew wasn't supposed to be crossed in the evening.

"I'm thinking we may need some help," Arlo said to his partner, as he flicked his cigarette across the road.

Ed nodded.

Arlo opened the pickup's door and grabbed two double barrel Parker shotguns from the gun rack mounted on the window behind the bench seat. He closed the door, and handed one to Ed. They simultaneously opened the breech of their shotguns to make sure they were loaded. They were. They snapped them shut again.

Jimbo, Roger, and Jackson got in front of Boyle and the men. “Y’all can’t go cross those tracks,” Roger pleaded.

The drunks pushed their way past him and continued slowly walking down the middle of the road.

Arlo and Ed walked toward the crossing. “Boys,” Arlo said loudly and evenly, “you’d better stop where you are. You ain’t got no business over here.”

Boyle stepped ahead of the others and stopped walking. “We’re going to the Twilight to get us a drink.”

“No you’re not,” Ed’s raspy voice answered.

Three of the service unit men pushed past Boyle. “And who’s gonna stop us?” One of them yelled across the tracks.

Arlo and Ed raised their shotguns to chest level, then Arlo answered. “Me, and my friends, Ed and Mr. Parker.

The three drunken service unit men and Boyle started walking again toward the crossing

“Mister, we got money,” Boyle pleaded. “All we want is a drink.”

Arlo aimed his shotgun at the ground in front of them and shot. No one was hit directly, but some of the birdshot ricocheted and hit the foursome.

Arlo and Ed aimed their guns higher and walked toward the tracks. When they were almost at the crossing, a loud shotgun blast sounded from behind Boyle and the service unit men. Arlo and Ed stopped.

Betty appeared beside Boyle carrying an old, large ten-gauge shotgun in her hands. "Arlo, Ed, I'll handle this."

They didn't move.

"You know me, and you know I ain't ever looking for no trouble. You have my word, I'll take care of these men."

Arlo and Ed stared at Betty for a long moment, and then Arlo lowered his shotgun. "Keep your niggers in line Betty, or we'll close you down, permanently."

"I told you, you have my word," Betty said angrily looking at Boyle.

The two cowboys turned around and walked to their pick-up. They looked back for a full minute before they opened the doors and re-hung their shotguns on the gun rack.

"Don't let this happen again, Betty." Arlo yelled across the tracks. Then he and Ed got in the truck and pulled away, burning rubber.

As soon as they left, Lulu, Billy, and Roger rushed forward to help the bloodied men,

Betty stared at the cut on Boyle's face and his bloodied arm. "You was mighty lucky tonight, but you pull that shit again, and *I'm* gonna shoot you before you ever get of out my door." She turned to leave, then twisted back to him with a scowl. "And next time my gun won't be loaded with no rock salt either."

Betty stopped next to Roger and pointed at the three service unit men who had gotten the worse of the ricocheting birdshot and gravel. "Get them inside. I'll help clean them up then I want you to take them home on the bus. They can get their cars tomorrow when they're sober, but I ain't gonna take no chances on anything else happening tonight."

"We'll take care of it, Betty," Roger replied. "And thanks for your help. That was about to get real ugly."

Boyle stood in the road, wavering, and trying to focus his eyes on his wounded arm. When he felt something warm run down his face, he reached up and touched his cheek. "Ouch."

"Sergeant Boyle!" A deep voice bellowed through the night air and made Boyle spin around toward the angry sound.

It was Tucker. He was furious as he got out of the passenger door of Lucille and slammed it shut. Morris and Terrance quickly got out of the driver's door and followed Tucker, leaving Pearl wearing a nightgown and robe alone in the backseat.

Tucker stopped when he was toe to toe with Boyle. "You are one stupid son of a bitch," he yelled and then leaned even closer to Boyle's face. "What the hell were you trying to do, get our men killed?"

Drunk and shaken, Boyle put his head down. He didn't answer or move.

Tucker took a deep breath and stepped back without taking his eyes off Boyle. "You get yourself and the men on the bus, and get back to the barracks."

"Yes, sir," Boyle replied softly.

Terrance ran to the bar door and motioned for Jimbo to come out. "You need to get the bus," Terrance said quietly. "We're going home. And we got to get the service unit men in there too."

Jimbo looked over Boyle and shook his head, then headed for the bus.

"I said get the men," Tucker said as he pushed Boyle toward the bar door. "Now."

Boyle walked through the door and thirty seconds later the rest of the Triple Nickles and the service unit men came out in a single file.

Jimbo opened the bus doors and everyone filed in.

Dixie waited until almost everyone had boarded the bus then walked up the Boyle and leaned close. "You ain't no leader, Sarge, you're nothing but a loser." Boyle looked at Dixie, but for once he didn't have anything else to say.

Roger and Jackson walked out of Betty's with their wives on their arm. They kissed them good-bye and were heading for the bus when Morris put his hand on Roger's shoulder. "Roger, I want you and Jackson to make sure that no one leaves the barracks again tonight."

"Yes, sir," Jackson replied.

"Yeah, We'll tuck 'em in." Roger assured him.

"Lulu, Billie," Morris called back to their wives, "Why don't you get in the car with Pearl? I'll take you back to Miss Rae's."

"Thank you, Lieutenant," Billie answered. "We'd appreciate that."

"How about you?" Morris turned and asked Tucker. "Can I give you a lift back?"

"I think I'll just take the bus, but thanks," Tucker said as he boarded the bus.

Morris slapped the side of the bus by the open doors, signaling Jimbo that all the passengers were on board.

Jimbo nodded, closed the doors, and slowly pulled away from Betty's Bar.

"That should be an interesting ride," Morris said to himself as he walked back to the *car.*

Lulu and Billie had already settled in the backseat, and were both talking at one time telling Pearl about Boyle, the two guys with shotguns, and Betty with her shotgun.

"And to think that all that happened while I was asleep in my bed with my husband snuggled up next to me. I'm really sorry I missed all the excitement," Pearl said sarcastically as she moved to the front seat.

"Well I can tell you..."

Morris opened the driver's door and scowled at the two women in the backseat.

Lulu and Billie looked at his face and stopped talking.

Pearl slid across the bench seat to get closer to her husband. She kissed him on the cheek, then put her head on his shoulder as he put the car in gear and headed back to Miss Rae's.

CHAPTER TWENTY

The large, round black-rimmed clock hanging on the front wall of the barracks read six forty-two when Terrance rushed through the screen door.

"Sweet Jesus," he said to himself as the smell of alcohol and cigarettes overwhelmed him. He ran to the squad room and looked around at a dozen half-dressed men lying haphazardly across their beds. Boyle was lying on top of a pile of clothes on the floor, snoring.

"Holy shit." He ran back to Tucker's door, and knocked. "Captain Freeman, Captain Freeman," he called loudly, banging on the door.

Tucker jerked opened the door as he continued to button his shirt. He was face to face with Terrance. "What the hell's going on, Terrance?"

"The cook in the officers' dining room just told me that Richardson had breakfast early 'cause he's gonna do a surprise inspection here this morning."

"Great," Tucker shook his head in disgust.

The screen door slammed behind Terrance, and Morris walked in. "I heard."

"OK, we gotta move fast," Tucker said excitedly. "Morris, get the men up, and cleaned up. Five minutes."

"Yes, sir."

"And Terrance, you and I are going to get this place looking spick and span in five minutes," Tucker said as he walked into the squad room. He stopped, shook his head, and then picked up a full ashtray and dumped it in a near by trashcan.

"If you say so, sir," Terrance replied, looking at the huge mess, "spick and span."

Morris shook Boyle and yelled loudly at the others. "Get your sorry asses up, now. You have one minute to hit the showers, and I want you dressed in four minutes."

Jimbo, Roger, Jackson, Dixie, and Willie had awaken when Terrance started banging on Tucker's door and were already headed for the showers in the back room.

The other men groaned, but didn't move to get up.

"In thirty seconds, I'm gonna take a stripe away from anyone still in bed," Morris yelled.

He kicked the pile of clothes Boyle was lying on. "And you're gonna lose two."

Blurry eyed, Boyle looked at Morris's angry face and without a word got up quickly and followed the other laggards to the showers.

Tucker picked up someone's duffel bag and began filling it with empty beer bottles and ashtray remains. When he finished he picked a white t-shirt off the floor, looked at it, shrugged then used it to wipe out all of the ashtrays and stacked them on the table in the back.

Terrance picked clothes off the floor, folded them and put them in neat stacks.

"Terrance, there isn't time for that," Tucker said. "Just pick all the clothes off the floor and take them to my room.

Terrance looked at Tucker questioningly, but gathered up an armload and followed Tucker to his room.

Tucker hurriedly pushed his dresser catty-corner. “Throw the clothes behind here,” Tucker said pointing to the space behind the dresser.

Terrance looked shocked, but dumped the armload as told.

Tucker patted Terrance on the back as they hurried back to the main room. “That was an old trick I learned from a boyhood friend who couldn’t play unless his room was picked up! Do the same with Morris’s dresser. Then throw all the trash behind it.”

“You got it, sir.” Terrance gave Tucker a mock salute, then said to himself, “I got to remember this one.”

Tucker and Terrance went back to the squad room. “How about taking that duffel bag full of beer bottles that shouldn’t have even been in the barracks and putting it in *Lucille’s* trunk while I help Morris make beds.”

“Yes, sir.” Terrance picked up the bag and headed for the door.

Tucker and Morris moved from bed to bed quickly making them ready for inspection with taunt blankets and mitered corners.

When Terrance came back he grabbed a broom and began sweeping the floor just as the men emerged from the shower room. When he finished, he swept the debris in a dustpan, walked to Tucker's room and threw the broom, dustpan and dirt behind Tucker's dresser on the pile of clothes. Then closed both NCO room doors. "I really like this way of cleaning," he said to himself smiling.

At exactly seven o'clock, the men heard a jeep pull up outside. Colonel Richardson, Lieutenant Nick Davis, and two MPs got out.

Richardson opened the barracks door and walked in.

Boyle stood up and called, "Atten-hut," loudly.

All the men quickly came to attention next to the footlockers in front of their beds.

Tucker walked forward and greeted Richardson with a smile. "Good morning, sir. We were just getting ready to go to breakfast. How can I help you?"

Richardson sneered. "Heard the men were out pretty late last night." He looked around and began walking down the aisle with Lieutenant Davis at his side. The two

MPs remained posted at the door. "Thought I'd better check to make sure everyone is OK."

Richardson stopped in front of Dixie. He looked up and down checking every button and fold in Dixie's uniform.

Tucker stepped next to Richardson. "The men weren't out that late, sir, and everyone's fine. But thank you for your concern."

Richardson ignored Tucker and continued to look at Dixie. Then he nodded toward his footlocker.

Dixie opened it and Davis came forward to look. The left side of the top tray held folded handkerchiefs, socks, ties and a shoe shine kit. The right side had writing paper, a pen, a razor, toothbrush, and other toiletry items. It was perfect. Davis lifted the top tray and checked the bottom. It had out of season clothes, undershirts, underwear, and towels. Everything was folded and arranged perfectly for inspection. The Lieutenant put the tray back and closed the footlocker.

Richardson nodded toward the bed. Davis ran his hand over the top, looked at the mitered corners, and then checked the distance the pillow sat from the turned-down edge of the sheet. Next he got down on his knees and checked the floor under Dixie's bed then turned his head to look under the one next to it. He stood up and nodded at Richardson. Everything was as it should be.

The pair moved on, checking every man, and randomly checking footlockers and beds. Nothing was out of place.

Davis walked to the back to check the showers, sinks, and latrines, while Richardson walked to the front of the barracks to where Boyle was standing.

"So, Sergeant, where'd you get that?" He asked as he touched the small cut on the side of Boyle's face.

"Cut myself shaving, sir."

"Really?" Richardson took a closer look. "Not at Betty's Bar?"

Before Boyle could answer, Tucker stepped forward and asked, "Would you like to have a look at the officers' rooms, sir?"

Terrance made a choking sound and Richardson spun around.

"Sorry, sir, dry throat," Terrance apologized and continued to stare straight ahead.

Davis walked back from the shower room and stopped next to Richardson. "Would you like me to check the officers' rooms, sir?"

Richardson looked from Tucker to Morris then the rest of the men. "No. I'm sure that won't be necessary," he finally answered. He turned face-to-face with Tucker and his sneer returned. "By the way Captain, aren't you running a little late for class today?"

"No, sir. Major Wesley gave the men some extra time to rest after..."

Richardson interrupted. "After you failed to get the gondola or bombs?" He moved closer to Tucker. "You boys can't follow a simple order, can you?"

Tucker stood his ground. "The fire was not *simple.* Sir."

"You had your orders, Captain, and you will be written up for your failure to follow..."

The barracks door opened, breaking the escalating tension in the room immediately.

Sawyer walked in between the two MPs. The top of his left arm was wrapped in gauze and he was holding his backpack at his right side.

The men, who were still standing at attention, looked at Sawyer out of the corner of their eyes, but didn't dare move.

Tucker walked up to him. "Corporal, welcome back. Are you doing okay?"

Sawyer looked around, puzzled by the presence of the MPs and Richardson. He set his backpack on the floor. "Yes, sir. Not bad," he answered, still staring at Richardson. He opened up the backpack and handed the two defused bombs he'd picked up in the valley to Tucker.

"Doc said that having those two defused bombs in my backpack probably saved me."

Tucker looked at the bombs for a long moment, then smiled. He handed them to Richardson. "For Headquarters...as ordered."

Richardson glared at Tucker. He handed the two cylinders to his lieutenant and without another word walked out the door. Davis and the two MPs hurriedly followed him.

"At ease, men," Tucker said as soon as the screen door closed.

Sawyer reached into the backpack again and pulled out the tools he'd gathered up. He winked at Jackson as he handed Jimbo the tools. "Here you go, Jimbo. And thanks for not killing Jackson."

"I'd never of done that. But thanks for bringing 'em back." He looked at the handful of tools, then added, "Guess you didn't get the pack though."

"You're a funny man, Jimbo," Sawyer said punching his arm gently.

"What happened to the back of your head?" Roger asked staring. "The red hair turned black,"

"That ain't my hair. It's where my hair was before it got burnt off. But the Doc said it would grow back normal."

Tucker and Morris moved aside, while the others quickly surrounded Sawyer and continued their barrage of questions.

"Well, this sure has been an exciting morning." Tucker said to Morris as they stood back and watched the men.

"Indeed it has. About as exciting as getting out of a warm bed at midnight to drive to Betty's Bar—then leaving without ever getting a beer."

Tucker laughed. "That reminds me, I had Terrance throw all the empty beer bottles in *Lucille's* trunk. We probably need to get them to the trashcan before the car starts smelling like Betty's."

Morris scrunched his face. "I'll take care of that it right now!" He scooted around the men and out the screen door.

Sawyer broke away from the other men and walked over to Tucker. "Captain, I heard you came back to get me and carried me out. Thank you."

"Corporal, I'm just happy you're OK. And I wish I had thought to pick up those bombs. So I'm the one that needs to thank you for your quick thinking." Tucker offered his hand, and Sawyer shook it. "Now why don't you get some rest, while we get our chores re-done."

Tucker looked at the rest of the men. "OK men, let's get this place cleaned up, spick and span." Then he turned to Terrance and winked. "Terrance, why don't you show them where all their clothes are. Then you can leave and start breakfast. We'll be in the mess hall in about an hour."

CHAPTER TWENTY-ONE

Doctor Silva stood at the front of the Hangar A classroom pointing to a contour map hanging on the wall with large, colorful magnetic shapes spread over it.

"The fire started here," he pointed to a large red circle, "caused by a lightning strike. The wind was blowing from the northeast," he pointed to a large blue directional arrow. "And we had teams fighting the fire and cutting fire breaks on the west and south sides of the fire," he continued to point, "here, here, and here. And, of course you all were just below the ridge, here."

Morris raised his hand. "Were you expecting the fire to spread to the gap south of the ridge we were on?"

"No. That was pretty unexpected. But a fire isn't always predictable, especially when the wind is constantly changing." Silva picked up a large red cardboard arrow. "Unfortunately the fire jumped one of the breaks before it was finished, and a new fire started to the south. The men there were really lucky they didn't get trapped. Then when the fire reached the gap, the wind changed again." Silva took the blue wind arrow and turned it 180 degrees. "That's when it moved through the gap and up the next valley—the one you were in." He looked from Tucker to his men. "And you know firsthand what happened then."

They all nodded.

The hangar door opened and Major Wesley walked to the front of the classroom and joined Silva.

"Sorry to interrupt."

He turned to the men. "I just got a call that a large white UFO was spotted by a private pilot flying over the Loma Linda area."

Silva walked to the back and rolled out a corkboard with two Forest Service maps pinned on it, while

Wesley continued. “If it’s really another intact Fu-Go, Richardson wants us to get the instruments in the gondola. And, of course, whatever bombs are attached. You know the drill.” He paused. “I think he’s in some kind of competition with the CO at Chico to see which base can collect more pieces for the Operation Field Office.” He shook his head and picked up the wooden pointer. “Anyway, the balloon is lying in a gulch in this area. As you can see, the terrain all around the gulch is steep and narrow, and rocky,” he said. He looked at Tucker and continued, “but nothing like the Wallowa Ridge. Another problem in the area is a large grove of two-hundred-foot ponderosa pines and Douglas firs just below the gulch that come up the southern side from the valley. Keep above that stand of trees and you’ll be fine.”

Wesley took a deep breath and looked at Silva with a worried look in his eyes, then turned back to face the men. “There is one other problem. There’s a severe storm with heavy rains and winds heading our way from the west, so we need to finish this mission as quickly as we can.”

Wesley looked at Jonesy who had taken to sitting in the last row during all of the briefings and debriefings. As usual he was chewing on a toothpick and rocking his chair on its two back legs. "Jonesy, keep your eyes on the weather and as soon as the last man is out, I want you to get back here, pronto."

"Yes, sir," he answered casually as he rocked forward putting all four legs on the floor.

"Lastly, I'll have a truck waiting to pick you up at the bottom of the mountain on this old logging road," he said pointing to a spot on the map. "Questions?"

Morris raised his hand. "Sir, do we need to take anything special...like longer let-down ropes, in case we do land in one of those trees?"

"I'll let Doctor Silva take that one." Wesley said looking to Silva for help.

"Sounds smart, Lieutenant," Silva replied, "but fifty-feet of rope is the maximum we have, and have ever jumped with." He paused and smiled. "You just really need to stay away from everything that's tall and green, and focus on gray and rocky instead."

The men chuckled and nodded.

"OK men," Wesley said, "like I said, we need to set up our jump as quickly as possible." Wesley looked around the classroom and pointed to men as he continued. "Boyle, Roger, Willie, and Jackson, you're jumping. I want you to do a site inspection as soon as you get to the balloon. Willie, you're communications man. Radio me with the condition of the gondola, and what components are attached."

"Yes, sir."

"And if your radio doesn't work in the gulch, send the bird," Wesley caught himself, "I mean Angel, back with the information."

Willie nodded as Angel cooed from his shoulder. She too had gotten in the habit of attending the briefings, sitting on his shoulder or walking around the hangar floor.

Wesley continued. "Sawyer, if you're up to it, you're jumpmaster."

"Will do, sir," Sawyer said nodding.

"Captain Freeman, you and Lieutenant Morris will coordinate from the tower. Everyone else with me, we need to make up a couple of new A-5s with bomb disposal equipment, foul weather gear, and extra rations, in case the weather delays your departure off the mountain."

Wesley stepped forward and handed Jonesy a sheet of paper. "The drop coordinates. Can you have the plane ready to go in twenty minutes."

"Can do." Jonesy slowly got up and sauntered to the door.

"And Jonesy," Wesley called after him, "watch the weather."

"Will do, sir."

Boyle, Jackson, and Roger stood inside the open door of the C-47's cargo, while Sawyer walked from man to man checking the main parachute on their back, the secondary chute on their front, the small front pack, and the webbed belt that held their let-down rope, canteen, and knife.

Willie stood on the tarmac ready to walk up the ladder of the C-47 when he heard Tucker call his name. He turned around.

"I just wanted to make sure you picked up one of the new radios that just came in," Tucker said when he got to Willie.

"Sure did," he answered looking down at all the equipment he was carrying. "It's here somewhere."

Not ready to go into her harness yet Angel was sitting on his shoulder bobbing and making cooing noises.

"And, of course you have your backup radio." Tucker smiled.

"Yeah. But she's acting mighty nervous. She squawks and fights every time I try to put her into the shoulder harness."

Tucker looked up at the darkening sky. "Probably knows that weather's coming."

He turned to Angel and said teasingly. "She's afraid she'll get her pretty feathers all wet and be mistaken for a drowned rat."

"Honestly, Captain, sometimes you're as bad as the rest of them, teasing Angel that way." Willie kissed her beak. "And you know she's the sweetest gal around here."

"Now that I do agree with!"

Jackson poked his head out of the C-47's door. "Willie, you going with us or not."

"Hold your chute, I'm coming." Willie started up the steps, then turned and waved at Tucker. "See you in the barracks."

"Angel, you hurry back too, sugar," Tucker called sweetly.

Willie harrumphed.

Angel cooed.

Tucker backed away from the plane, when the marshaller took his place on the tarmac in front of the plane and signaled the pilot to start his engines.

A moment later the left propeller slowly began to turn, and was soon followed by the right propeller.

The ground crew stepped in to remove the wooden blocks around the plane's wheels and were about to push the steps out of the way when a loud excited voice cut through the sound of the plane's engines.

"Wait!"

It was Silva's voice. He smiled as he ran past Tucker. "Looks like a great day for flying. Thought I'd go along for the ride."

Silva hit two of the five steps on the rollaway and disappeared inside the door of the C-47. The ground crew moved the steps back and out of the way as soon as Silva cleared them.

The marshaller walked backwards in front of the plane waving his arms for the plane to follow. When he stepped aside he motioned Jonesy to keep going. The plane taxied down the runway, ready for takeoff.

Tuckered waved at the departing plane then ran toward the apron and control tower. He met Morris at the edge of the runway, and together they headed to the control tower.

"I feel a lot better now that Doctor Silva's onboard," Morris said climbing the tower steps.

"I do too," Tucker said as he looked up at the darkening sky. "But I sure don't feel good about that sky."

CHAPTER TWENTY-TWO

Pendleton Field's control tower was a twelve by twelve glass room that sat squarely in the middle of the roof of the two-story cinderblock flight office building.

The rooftop room allowed a 360-degree view of the runways in front of the building, the two pair of Quonset hangars that sat on each side of it, and the skeletal base behind it.

It had taken the Army Corps of Engineers six months between 1941 and 1942 to turn Pendleton's existing municipal airport into a base that would house, feed and service the 2,500 personnel who would soon be stationed there.

And look at it now, Tucker thought as he looked around. *It's a ghost town.*

He poured the last drops of coffee from a pot that had been setting on a hot plate and walked over to the console.

"Bravo, this is Tower One, you're cleared for takeoff," Morris said into the microphone. He released the "on" button then looked at the clock above the window and noted the time in a logbook that sat open on the console in front of him.

Tucker watched the C-47 taxi down the runway, lift-off, and then climb into the graying sky until it finally disappeared in the clouds.

"I'd offer you some coffee," he said turning to Morris, "but it boiled down to one cup," He held his mug out. "I'm happy to share though."

Morris grimaced. "No thanks, Captain."

Tucker set the mug down and looked at the instrument panel on the console. "The barometric pressure is still dropping."

Morris checked the barometer. "It sure is." He made another note in the logbook.

"Radio Sawyer and find out how the weather looks from up there." Tucker said as he continued to stare at the darkening sky. "And make sure he's doing OK. I'm not sure he was ready to be flying so soon."

"He wanted to do it." Morris said as he turned the microphone on. "Bravo, this is Tower One, do you read me?"

Static noises sounded through the wall speakers in the tower for a few seconds, then Sawyer's voice came through. "Affirmative, Tower One. We got a lot of static, but I can hear you."

"How's the weather?" Morris asked.

"Sunny to the right, dark to the left, so Jonesy's leaning right."

"Make sure you and Jonesy keep an eye on that storm front. The barometer is still dropping."

"Will do, Lieutenant."

"The captain wants to know if you're doing OK."

"Tell him not to worry, I'm fine."

The tower door opened and Colonel Richardson and Lieutenant Davis walked in.

"Drop site ETA 10 minutes," Sawyer's voice continued over the speaker. "If we can, Jonesy and Silva want to do a pass at three hundred feet to see what the area looks like then get back up to twelve hundred to drop the A-5s and the men. Silva really wants to get the men on the ground before the weather hits."

Tucker gave Morris a "thumbs up".

"Bravo, let us know when you reach the drop site."

Davis walked up to the console and looked out of the tower window at the dark storm clouds on the horizon. "Doesn't look that bad."

Morris glared at the lieutenant and pointed to one of the gauges on the panel. "That's how you tell what the weather is doing and it says the wind's picking up," he frowned. "And worse, it's shifting."

Richardson came forward and stood next to Tucker. "The Field Office is expecting to get the instruments on that gondola—if your boys do their job."

"As long as the wind and rain cooperate, my *men* will get them."

Richardson leaned on the console, close to Tucker's face. "I know you colored boys don't like to get wet, but see if you can't do your job right this time," he hissed quietly. "You hear me?"

"Loud and clear."

Morris realized he still had the microphone when Silva's voice came booming over the speaker. "Tower One, this is Bravo, please remind the Colonel that we're not supposed to jump if the wind is blowing more than fifteen miles per hour. It's not safe."

"Doctor Silva," Richardson barked as he grabbed the microphone, "what in the hell are you doing on that plane?"

"Helping your men."

"My ass! This is an army mission. I'm in charge and will decide if they jump or not, not the Forest Service."

"Well, sir, in case you didn't know it, the army and the Forest Service have the same regulations concerning safe conditions for parachuting."

Richardson turned the microphone off, slammed it on the console, and looked at Lieutenant Davis. "Who does he think he is? Tomorrow, I want you to tell Major Wesley that I don't want Silva on any more flights unless I personally approve it."

"Yes, sir," Davis said jumping to attention.

CHAPTER TWENTY-THREE

The turbulence from the approaching storm made air pockets in the atmosphere that tossed and bounced the C-47 with so much force that Boyle, Jackson, Roger, and Willie had given up trying to talk to each other. Instead each man hung on to the long canvas bench seat opposite the jump door plane and tried to steady their bodies so they wouldn't embarrasses themselves by getting air sick.

Silva was lying on the left side of the open jump door trying to see the ground through the wispy gray clouds that had begun to get heavier and darker.

"Doctor Silva," Jonesy's voice boomed through the speaker next to the door. "We're about five miles from the target area. I'm going down closer." Silva grabbed the microphone next to him and turned it on.

"Sounds good. Ask Sawyer to bring me two wind streamers. I'll drop them as soon as you tell me we're at twelve hundred feet over the target. They should let us know what we're dealing with."

"Will do, but I'm going to try to get a lot closer to take a look."

"This isn't "the Hump" Jonesy, make sure you clear the mountaintop by more then a couple of feet, please."

"I'll try, sir."

A minute later, Sawyer walked up from the cockpit and knelt down next to Silva. He handed him two rolls of weighted wind streamers.

Jonesy's voice came over the speaker. "Target in thirty seconds. Altitude twelve hundred feet."

Silva dropped the first streamer and watched the wind whip it back and forth as it descended. "I don't know about this." He shook his head. "I'll bet the wind is gusting more than fifteen miles an hour on the ground."

Sawyer was watching the red ribbon toss back and forth toward the ground when he saw the same chasm on the mountainside that he'd seen on the map. "There's the gulch," he said excitedly, pointing to a long ravine off the left side of the plane.

Silva leaned on his elbows and raised the pair of binoculars that were strapped around his neck and looked. "Yup. And I can see our UFO—an intact Fu-Go about three-quarters up the east side of that big gulch."

Jonesy was back on the speaker. "I heard. I'm going in to give you a closer look. One pass then we're out of there and back up."

Sawyer continued to look as the plane banked around to get in closer. "It's gonna be a hard jump—only big boulders, rocks and scrub brush."

"I agree." Silva sat up and let the binoculars fall to his chest. "It really looks like our jump site options are pretty limited." Silva turned to Sawyer. "Where do you think we should try to make the drop zone?"

Sawyer was notably surprised by Silva's question. No white man had ever asked him for his opinion about anything. He immediately considered the terrain and the wind streamers then confidently answered Silva. "Right now the wind direction makes the scrub brush just above the balloon the best choice. It's going to be a lot easier for the men to scoot down hill rather then haul their stuff up the hill. The northern rim of the gulch also looked a little less rugged than the gulch itself or either side options."

Silva thought about it for a few moments, then smiled. "I agree." He picked up the microphone. "Jonesy, we're going to drop the A-5s next pass. See if you can get us about half-a-mile uphill from the gulch." Silva clicked the mike off and turned to Sawyer. "If the wind stays consistent that should put the A-5s in a tight area inline with the Fu-Go."

"I'll get the A-5s and the men ready."

The plane circled the area and continued to climb. When it reached twelve hundred feet, Jonesy leveled it off and announced he was circling the drop zone.

Sawyer signaled the men to move the A-5s to the door. When they had the equipment lined up, he attached the static line to the parachute webbing straps on the top of each duffel bag to the plane's center rod.

Silva stood beside the door watching the ground. When they were over the drop zone he signaled the men to push the first A-5 out. Three seconds later the parachute opened with a loud "woof". The next two A-5s followed right behind.

Silva and Sawyer stood on each side of the open door and watched the bags being tossed by an increasingly gusty wind that pushed them downhill well below the Fu-Go.

"Shit." Sawyer shook his head. "The wind sure ain't cooperating today."

"So much for a plan." Silva shrugged. "Tell the men we'll try to get them as close to the A-5s as we can but now they're going to have to trudge uphill to the balloon." He shook his head. "Honestly, I'm still not sure we should even be jumping."

"I'll tell them, but I know the men and they'll want to try to do it. They think they have something to prove to the colonel."

"Sawyer, don't you ever believe any of you have anything to prove to that fool. And I'm real close to calling this off, no matter what Richardson says or does to me."

"Thanks, Doctor," Sawyer smiled and continued. "I'll tell the men what happened with the A-5s."

Silva nodded as Sawyer turned to his four friends and knelt down in front of their jump seat.

They moved closer to hear over the loud cabin noise.

"We tried to get the A-5s in the area above the balloon, but the winds are crazy. The equipment is spread out all over below the balloon," Sawyer told them. "There's nothin' but rocks and brush around them so there ain't no good landing site nearby. Silva's thinking about aborting the jump cause the wind is right on the edge of not being safe. If it doesn't hit the max and y'all want to try we'll try to get all four of you down next pass."

Boyle looked at the others and gave them a thumbs up. Everyone nodded.

"We can do it," Boyle told Sawyer confidently.

"OK."

Silva saw what was going on and walked to where the men were huddled. "In this wind, you can probably expect to get dragged across some nasty rocks. Make sure your helmets are tight." The men checked their helmets and gave him the 'OK' signal.

Jonesy's voice came on the speaker. "One minute."

"Good luck." Sawyer tapped each man on his helmet, stood and then called, "Stand up and hook up."

The men hooked up their static lines.

"Stand in the door." Sawyer called out loudly.

The four men lined up, left foot forward.

Silva was lying down on the left side of the doorway, watching the ground. When the plane was over the jump site, Silva tapped Jackson's left leg. He jumped and seconds later his chute opened.

Roger lined up at the door and waited for the signal.

Third in line, Boyle turned around to Willie. "I got a lot to make up for, Willie," Boyle said sincerely. "I'm gonna get that gondola equipment for the captain to give the colonel, no matter what I have to do!"

"I'll help you, Sarge, no matter what *we* have to do," Willie smiled. "We'll get it done."

Roger jumped.

Boyle stepped into the doorway and Silva tapped his left leg. He jumped.

Willie stepped up to the open door.

Silva stood up and put his arm across the door in front of Willie. "Wait a minute." He turned to Sawyer.

"The wind is picking up, and it's veering in the gulch." He looked out the door again as the plane circled. "Roger and Jackson aren't close, and I think Boyle is going to be even further away from the target." He grabbed the microphone. "Jonesy, I've got one more jumper. Would you make one more pass? I want to check the wind again before I let Willie jump."

"You got it," Jonesy's voice answered.

Silva looked at Sawyer. "I don't like what I'm seeing. The wind has picked up and it's not safe. I think we should let the tower know that Willie probably won't be jumping."

Sawyer walked to the cockpit, took the co-pilot seat on the right of the plane, put the headset on, switched the overhead toggle to radio and turned the microphone on.

"Tower One, this is Bravo, come in."

"Bravo, this is Tower One," Morris replied, "what's your status?"

"The wind is over the limit, and Silva says it's not safe. We have three men spread all over the mountainside. We're making a second pass now, to get a closer look but it's doubtful that Willie will be able to jump in this wind."

"This is Colonel Richardson." Richardson's voice boomed over the headsets so loudly that both Jonesy and Sawyer pulled their headsets away from their ears. "What the hell do you mean that he might not be jumping? I want his black ass on the ground next pass. Do you hear me?"

"Sir, Doctor Silva and I ..."

"Goddamn it. Silva does not speak for the army. I am in charge of this mission, and you have one simple goddamn job. I want that man on the ground and those goddamn instruments brought back here. You understand me?"

"Yes, sir, we'll do what..." Sawyer heard a click and thought Richardson had turned his microphone off, but then he heard Richardson yell at Tucker.

"You're their goddamn leader, tell them to do their job, that's an order."

"Yes, sir," Tucker replied, as a door slammed in the background.

Sawyer heard Tucker ask Morris to try to get Bravo on the radio again, and Sawyer piped in. "Tower One your microphone's been on. We heard Richardson."

"Sawyer, if there's anyway to get Willie down, try." Tucker's voice beseeched. "But if it's not safe, don't let him jump. I'll take full responsibility."

"We'll do our best, sir. Sawyer took the headset off, hooked it next to the copilot seat, and stood to leave.

"Richardson is one ass," Jonesy said shaking his head.

"He sure is," Sawyer agreed, and walked to the back of the plane, disgusted.

Silva was standing by Willie at the door. He looked from the speaker to Sawyer. "We heard, too."

Jonesy's voice came over the speaker. "Target in one minute. And just so you know, the wind is gusting at seventeen, and it's started to rain."

"What do you think?" Sawyer quietly asked Silva.

"Let's see what it looks like when we get there."

Sawyer lifted the cabin's headset and turned the microphone on. "Tower One, this is Bravo. Thirty seconds to target. The wind is increasing."

"Do it if you can," Tucker said, and hesitated. "But I don't want..."

Willie with Angel in his shoulder harness moved closer to the door. "What do'ya think, sugar?" Willie asked Angel. Angel cooed. "I agree. Let's go help the Sarge."

Willie leapt out of the door.

Stunned, Sawyer dropped the radio. He moved next to Silva in the open door. They watched as Willie's parachute open, a strong gust of wind quickly carried him away.

Sawyer picked up the radio and shouted excitedly. "Willie jumped. The wind is sheering and it looks like it's dragging him straight for the bottom of the mountain."

"Shit!" Tucker's voice boomed back.

The plane began to rock and bounce fiercely from the turbulence.

"Hey, we need to get out of here," Jonesy yelled from the cockpit. "The storm front is here and I'm getting real uncomfortable!"

Silva and Sawyer felt the plane turn and climb higher. They continued to look out of the open door watching the ground disappear into a heavy fog as the wind driven rain pounded harder.

CHAPTER TWENTY-FOUR

Torrents of rain fell, assaulting Willie's face as he dangled between two broken Douglas fir branches. His uniform had torn when he fell through branches higher in the tree, and become stained dark by a mixture of pine resin and blood.

He'd lost his helmet somewhere in the fall, and his face and hands were crisscrossed by scrapes and cuts. Rivulets of blood mixed with rainwater coursed down his face and from a deep gash in his left arm below his elbow.

He tried to look up through the pelting rain but couldn't see where his parachute was caught. When he slowly turned his head to the side he saw that he was about six feet from the trunk of the tree. He looked down but didn't see the ground.

Angel was in his shoulder harness, but not moving.

"I'm sorry, Sugar," he whispered weakly, "I know you don't like the rain."

Willie lifted his right hand and tried to grab a branch and work his way over to the trunk, but the shrouds of his parachute were tangled above him, making it impossible to move.

"Well, Sugar, it looks like we're gonna have to get ourselves free of this chute if we wanna get down."

Using only one hand, Willie found the end of the let-down rope hanging from the web belt hooked at his waist. He pulled the end free from the rest of the looped rope and brought it up, close to his face.

"OK," he said softly to himself, "we practiced this, not one-handed, but I can do it." He put the end of the rope through his harness ring and looked for a branch to throw it over. He took a breath. He was hurt and exhausted. And he didn't see a branch that wasn't tangled with the shroud lines.

"I can do this," he told himself again, as he looked up to let the driving rain wash the blood away from his eyes. "Maybe I can tie the let-down line through a shroud line ring. What do you think, Sugar?"

Angel didn't respond.

"Well, you may not think it'll work, but if the chute is caught real good up there, it'll work." He reached up and found the two shroud line rings above his head and tried to tie a good one-handed knot. "Angel, when we get back, you need to remind me to tell Doctor Silva that they need to make tying knots with one hand part of the training."

When he was satisfied with his knot he reached down to his waist and unhooked the other end of the let-down rope. It dropped toward the ground. He suddenly felt lighter, and a little better.

He looked at Angel. She still wasn't moving. "Hang on tight, Sweetheart. I know you don't like this part, but I need to take the chute harness off."

Using his right arm to hang onto the rope, Willie weakly pulled himself up slightly to release the tension on the harness. When he succeeded, he disconnected the harness and slipped out of it. Exhausted, he hung onto the let-down rope and rested.

The wind picked up and the tree began to sway.

Willie clung tighter to the rope and desperately looked around for a branch that he could get to, but the rain pelted his face and he couldn't keep his eyes open.

Suddenly a gust of wind whipped the tree, loosening the parachute from the top branches. The chute slid downward ten feet then jerked to a stop. And Willie's hands slid down the wet rope until he couldn't hang on any more.

He and Angel fell downward, quickly gaining momentum through one hundred and twenty-feet of thick Douglas fir branches until their battered, dead bodies hit the ground.

CHAPTER TWENTY-FIVE

Alone in the barracks, Tucker stood by Willie's bed and Angel's empty landing box. He pounded the wall next to the window opening with his fist as tears rolled down his cheeks.

Terrance came in the barracks carrying a tray of food. He walked to the back of the squad room and set it down on the card table in the corner. "Captain," he said softly. "I hoped you might like a roast beef sandwich and some hot coffee."

"I'm not hungry, Terrance, but thanks." Tucker walked away from the window and sat down on one of the card table chairs.

Terrance moved the tray of food closer. "You need to eat, sir."

Tucker stared into space. "Terrance, I have never felt a hurt like this in my life. Why? Why did it have to happen to Willie? To Angel? No one should have died trying to get some damn balloon in a storm."

"We're all feelin' the hurt, sir," Terrance said sadly. "Willie and Angel were sure special."

"If only I'd said 'no' to Richardson. I shouldn't have followed his orders. He's a mean spirited bastard. He doesn't belong in the army." Tucker paused and shook his head. "But neither do I."

"It wasn't your fault. You know you have to follow orders. Remember—that's why they're call *orders*," Terrance countered using Tucker's catchphrase. "Besides, Silva and Sawyer weren't going to let him jump anyway. They knew the wind was too strong. Willie knew it, but he just up and jumped on his own." Terrance shook his head. "It wasn't anybody's fault but his."

"Terrance, the men in the platoon haven't liked me since I got here. And now they must hate me. I just wanted..."

The barracks door opened and Major Wesley walked in.

Terrance stood up and looked at Tucker. "Eat. I'll come back later for the tray, and I expect to see a clean plate." He started to leave and turned back. "Captain the men don't hate you. It's just you that hates yourself right now. And for no good reason." He walked toward the door.

When he passed Wesley they both slowed, sharing a conspiratorial look. "I keep trying to get him to eat," Terrance said quietly to Wesley as he passed. "But it ain't happening yet, sir."

Wesley nodded as Terrance without a missed step kept heading for the door.

Wesley pulled up a chair and sat down across the table from Tucker.

"Tucker, you need to get out of here."

"I was thinking the same thing, sir," Tucker said with his head down, looking at his hands folded on the table. "I hoped I could be a part of the camaraderie my men enjoyed, and maybe even be the kind of leader my grandfather was," he said shaking his head, "but neither one of those are ever going to happen." He paused reflectively then added, "The army, these men deserve more. They'll all be better off without me. You're right, I need to get out of here."

Wesley sat, thunderstruck. "What!" he finally yelled. "I meant that you need to get out of the barracks, not leave the platoon. You've been sitting in here long enough feeling sorry for yourself." Wesley pushed back from the table and stood up. "Your men need you, and I think you need them. I want to see you back in Hangar A at 1300."

Tucker stood. "Sir, I want to be reassigned."

Wesley's face grew dark with anger. He leaned his fists on the table and stared at Tucker. "Oh sure, give Richardson what he wants. He'd love to transfer you. He's said all along that the Triple Nickles shouldn't be in the army. Shouldn't be paratroopers. They don't have what it takes. Now you want to prove him right?"

"Morris can take over. He should have been their company commander anyway," Tucker countered. "The men can stay together with him as their officer."

Wesley angrily walked to the door, then stopped abruptly and turned around. "Tucker, if you want a transfer, you go talk to Richardson. But your grandfather and the other Buffalo Soldiers were heroes and an inspiration to others because they didn't quit, no matter what."

"I've never tried to be a Buffalo Soldier."

"Nor have you ever believed you might just be more of an inspiration to your men than your grandfather was to his men—and you." Wesley headed for the door again. "And you're wrong about something else too. From what I hear, your men think a hellava lot more of you than you think of yourself."

Hazel opened the door to come in just as Wesley was leaving.

"Hangar A, 1300," he yelled without looking back. "That's an order, Captain."

"Yes, sir," Tucker answered quietly.

"Did you get ahold of her?" Wesley asked Hazel in a whisper.

She nodded as she stepped inside past him. They exchanged a smile as she continued to walk toward Tucker.

"Captain, someone named Dorothy called to find out how you were doing. She said she was your fiancée. And she's been concerned since she talked to you yesterday."

"I hung up on her."

Hazel crinkled her nose. "That wasn't nice."

"Hazel, I don't need one more person telling me that what happened to Willie and Angel is over and I need to let it go. I can't. I'm responsible for Willie's death. Me. How can I move on?"

"By learning from his example," Hazel sat down in the chair across from Tucker. "You know everyone we meet in our life is a teacher. Some like Richardson are negative, but they still have something to teach—how not to act! Others like Willie show us the positive influence we can have. He had an innocence and an infectious happiness that made everyone feel better—something we should all strive to do, maybe."

Tucker stared at his hands and didn't answer.

After a few moments, Hazel pushed the chair back and stood.

"I promised Dorothy I'd have you call her back. Why don't you stop by the office before you go to the hangar?

“Would you please have the paperwork to request a reassignment ready for me when I stop by,” Tucker asked with his head still down.

Hazel let out an audible sigh. “Sorry, that’s not a form I keep on hand. But I’ll request one from headquarters. It should be here in a couple of days.”

She turned and left.

CHAPTER TWENTY-SIX

Silva was sitting on the corner of the table talking to the men about the effects of wind shear on parachutes and fires, when Tucker opened the hangar door and walked to the front.

Silva stopped talking and the sixteen men facing him turned around and watched Tucker somberly walk to their makeshift classroom.

"Captain, thank you for joining us," Silva said. "We were just talking about wind shear."

Tucker remained standing by his empty chair. "Sir, I just came to tell you and the men that I've decided..." He stopped and turned as he heard the hangar door open behind him.

Colonel Richardson walked in.

All of the men stood at attention as he passed, heading for the front table. Lieutenant Davis had to walk more briskly than usual to keep up with him.

Major Wesley followed the duo carrying a large map rolled up under his arm. "Take a seat with your men, Captain," Wesley told Tucker quietly, but firmly as he passed.

Davis slowed when he overheard Wesley's comment and turned around to look at both of the men with a puzzled expression on his face.

Tucker sat down next to Morris.

"Doctor Silva," Richardson said as he joined Silva at the table. "We've been asked to help prevent a potentially catastrophic situation." He let his words sink in for a moment, then continued. "Major Wesley will brief you in a minute, but I want to make sure you boys understand something," he said as he looked at the faces seated in front of him, "I am in charge of this mission and I expect you to follow my orders, to the letter...." His voice trailed off as the hangar door opened again. It was Hazel. Her high heels tapped quickly as she almost ran to the front.

"Goddamn it, Hazel," Richardson yelled.

"It's not polite to curse at a lady, Colonel," Hazel said breathlessly as she reached the front. "General Garrett needs to talk to you right away." Then she asked mischievously, "Or should I tell him you're in a meeting, again?"

Hazel arched her eyebrow, tossed her gum in the nearby trashcan, then crossed her arms and stared at Richardson whose face was bright red with anger.

Nick rushed forward. "I can take the call for you, sir"

Hazel uncrossed her arms and glared at Nick. "Oh, really? The Colonel is too busy, but his lieutenant isn't." She turned to leave. "I'll let the general know."

"Hazel," Richardson's voice boomed, "you stay right there and don't say another word." He calmed himself and continued. "I just need a minute to finish with the boys. Then I'll be there."

"OK, Colonel, I'll go tell General Garrett to hang on—you're busy with *the boys*."

"Jesus Christ, Hazel! I'm coming!"

Richardson leaned over to whisper something to Wesley, as Hazel spun around to leave.

She slowed next to Tucker and met his sad eyes. "Learn from him. Don't let him win," she said with a tender smile. She squeezed his shoulder softly, picked up her pace again and walked quickly toward the door.

Richardson picked his hat up from the table, motioned Davis forward, and headed to the door after Hazel. When he was next to Tucker, he briefly looked his way and said loudly. "And this time you'd better get it done...right."

Richardson and Davis caught up with Hazel just as she opened the door. "And you shouldn't use the Lord's name in vain, either," she scolded.

Wesley stood quietly at the front shaking his head watching the trio leave. "OK, men, time to get serious. We really don't have time to waste." He handed the map he'd brought with him to Silva, who immediately tacked it to the corkboard and rolled it forward.

Wesley picked up the pointer and tapped the map. "This is Hanford Engineering Works on the Columbia River in Washington. It's a top secret government site for something called the Manhattan Project." He looked at the men. "I don't know what they're doing there, but I've been told that what they're working on will end the war."

The Triple Nickles looked at each other, absorbing the good news, and smiled at Wesley.

Tucker sat quietly, unfazed.

Wesley continued, "Unfortunately, a balloon has landed on one of their power lines causing a power outage. They have a three-hour backup system at their substation," he said as he pointed to the map. "And from what I've been told, if the power isn't restored to the facility, well…" he said gravely, "…it will be catastrophic for the US instead of Japan.

Wesley turned to Silva. "Bill, would you roll the board with the Fu-Go schematic up here, too."

Silva nodded and quickly moved the schematic next to the aerial map.

"The balloon was seen floating above the facility about thirty minutes ago. Then fifteen minutes ago the substation reported a power loss along the entire L27 line," Wesley said tracing the line on the aerial map. "That line provides 230 kilovolts of power to one of the three sections of Hanford that's working on the secret project." Wesley turned back to the men. "This is where it gets real tricky because if that bomb goes off, more than likely it'll take out part of the power line and they'll never be able to get the power for that section restored in time."

Wesley looked at his watch. "According to my watch, we've got two hours and thirty minutes to get there, find the balloon, defuse the bomb or bombs, figure out how the balloon is causing the line to short out, and fix it." Wesley paused and looked at the men. "I've been thinking about how the balloon could have caused the power loss and short, and I really don't know, but I am pretty sure if the Fu-Go caused the power loss it has to have something to do with the metal ring or the gondola, so after you defuse the bomb, check both of them."

Morris raised his hand. "And I suppose Richardson wants the balloon and instruments brought back for the Operation Field Office."

"Of course," Wesley replied, and then continued ominously. "But if you don't get the power restored, you won't need to worry about the balloon or anything else."

Morris looked at him for a long moment. "Understood."

Wesley picked up a clipboard from the table. "OK, assignments. I don't know how many it'll take to get the balloon off the line, so everyone will be jumping. I'll stay here and coordinate with the Hanford substation. Doctor Silva, you're jumpmaster. Morris get the A-5s ready and onboard."

Wesley looked up and searched the faces in front of him until he found Jimbo, then he continued. "Jimbo, you're our electrical man, make sure all the tools you need, or think you could possibly use, are packed."

"Yes, sir," Jimbo replied proudly, "You don't need to worry 'bout that. I've always got my tools together, in shape, and ready to go." He turned to Jackson and added, "And they'll be staying with me this time."

Jackson grimaced as the other men chuckled.

Jimbo turned back to Wesley and asked, "Ain't nobody from the power company gonna help?"

"No, unfortunately," Wesley frowned. "Because the balloon is really a bomb, it's all ours. But there will be a lineman at the substation to walk us through any line problems or answer any question, and I'll have an open line to him."

Morris raised his hand. "And what if the balloon is in the middle of a line run, how are we gonna get to it?"

"We're trying to rundown a couple of bosun chairs like the regular linemen use," Wesley answered. "But so far we can't find any that are close enough to Hanford or here." He turned to Silva. "So if we can't get any here in time, I'm counting on Jimbo and Doctor Silva to come up with an alternative."

Silva and Jimbo exchanged puzzled looks.

Wesley looked at his watch again. "OK, we've got a lot to do and the clock is ticking. Let's move."

Tucker lagged behind as the rest of his men headed to the door. When they were out of earshot he walked up to Wesley. "Permission to stay behind, sir."

"Permission denied, Captain," Wesley answered sternly. "And before you join *your* men on the plane, stop by the barracks and tell Terrance I'll need his help in the tower."

Tucker stood quietly for a moment then answered. “Yes, sir.” Deflated he turned and headed for the hangar door.

Wesley looked at Silva, who was gathering up the maps on the table and said, “Keep an eye on him, Bill.”

“Will do.” Silva put the maps under his arm and started for the door.”

“And just for your information, Hanford is making plutonium and if we don’t get the power back on…well, let’s just say that this is probably the most critical mission you and I will ever have.”

Silva shook his head at the news and whistled.

“Good luck, Bill. I want to see everyone back here.”

Silva gave Wesley a mock salute with the rolled maps, and left the hangar.

PART 4: HANFORD

CHAPTER TWENTY-SEVEN

For once, the C-47 wasn't bouncing in the turbulence and making the plane's metal frame groan with its usual deafening noises. But the relative quietness in the cabin didn't inspire conversation amongst the sixteen Triple Nickles seated on the long jump seats either. Everyone, but Jimbo, sat in silence and lost in thought.

Jimbo sat at the far end of the jump seat with his tools spread out beside him, working to bend hooks on a parachute harness with a pair of pliers.

Doctor Silva stepped out of the cockpit where he'd been talking to Jonesy and Morris, and walked past the silent men as he headed toward Jimbo.

"How's it going?" he asked.

Jimbo held out the parachute harness he'd modified. "A lineman's harness...instead of a bosun chair. I added a strap to put over the line."

Silva took it, inspected it carefully, and finally looked at Jimbo and smiled. "Yeah. This will work. See if you can make at least one more...two more if there's time and parts."

He handed the harness back and patted Jimbo on the shoulder. "You're really something, you know that?"

Jimbo smiled proudly.

Silva turned and walked back down the line of men until he stood in front of Tucker. "Captain Freeman, join me at the door."

Tucker set his helmet on the jump seat and followed him to the door. Silva picked up a pair the binoculars and hung them around his neck, then got a second pair out of a cubbyhole beside the door and handed them to Tucker. "We've just entered the Hanford airspace and are looking for the substation somewhere in the southeast quadrant."

Hanford Engineering Works occupied 670 square miles in south-central Washington where it was bounded by Saddleback Mountain, Rattlesnake Hills, and the Columbia River.

In 1942, when the Army Corps of Engineers determined the site met the government's criteria—an isolated wasteland far from any population centers and an area with an abundant supply of cold water—the Corps contracted the Du Pont Company to begin construction of a facility there. In 1943, when the site became operational, it joined Oak Ridge, Tennessee and Los Alamos, New Mexico, as part of the super-secret Manhattan Project. By February 1945, when the first refined plutonium was delivered to Los Alamos, the Hanford site had three nuclear reactors, three plutonium processing facilities, more than five hundred buildings, 350 miles of roads, 150 miles of railroad tracks, and 185 miles of electrical power lines.

Tucker lifted the binoculars and carefully scanned the horizon until he saw an isolated white cinderblock building enclosed by high fencing in the distance.

Tucker tapped Silva and pointed to the building.

Silva looked. He saw it and picked up the radio. "Jonesy," he said into the microphone. "We can see the substation ninety degrees west. The balloon is supposed to be a couple of miles east of the station, so follow the lines just ahead of us."

"Yes, sir," Jonesy's voice came over the speaker. "Eastward we go…like the wind."

The plane banked right sharply. Tucker and Silva grabbed the doorframe while the other men hung on to their seats.

"Damn." Silva shook his head. "I guess once you flown the Hump, you have to do something to make flying over plains fun."

As the C-47 flew over the power lines, Jonesy brought it back to horizontal and followed the power lines like a car driving on the highway.

Silva grabbed the microphone again. "That was fun," he said sarcastically, and then asked, "Can you take us a little lower?"

"You got it," Jonesy said. The plane quickly descended.

"Doctor Silva," Morris called through the speaker, "I think you need to get up here. There's a lot of smoke ahead of us."

Silva hesitated and looked at Tucker.

"Go ahead," Tucker said. "I'll keep looking for the balloon."

"Thanks." Silva put the radio down and hurried to the cockpit.

Silva stood between Jonesy and Morris in the cockpit, watching gray clouds of smoke billow up from the ground in front of them.

The wind gusted on the ground, pushing the smoke lower for a second.

"Holy shit. What the hell is..." Silva started to ask as he pointed out the cockpit window. Then he realized he already knew the answer to his question. "Looks like we found our Fu-Go."

Jonesy and Morris followed Silva's gaze and saw what looked like a huge white sheet draped over the power lines on the ground ahead of them.

"But a fire sure adds a new wrinkle to our plan." Silva turned to Morris, "Let Major Wesley know."

Morris picked up the headset and flipped the overheard radio toggle switch.

"Tower One, this is Bravo, come in."

"Bravo, this is Tower One. What's going on?" Wesley's voice answered.

"We found the balloon, Major," Morris replied. "It's on the power line about two miles east of the substation, and we've got a brush fire that looks like it started under the balloon and is moving northeast."

"Is the fire going to be a problem for you?" Wesley asked.

"We don't think so, sir. Right now it's moving away from the area, but we're going to drop the firefighting equipment just to be..." Morris was interrupted by a clicking sound and then muffled voices through the speaker. He looked at Jonesy and shrugged.

Jonesy shook his head back. He didn't know what was going on.

Richardson's voice suddenly boomed through the speaker. "Where's the captain?"

"In the cabin with the men," Morris replied.

"Well, I want you to remind him that getting that balloon off the wire and back here is your only job," Richardson said, his voice booming louder. "Don't you waste time unpacking an A-5 for a fire that isn't even there!"

"Yes, sir. Over and out," Morris said, flipping the radio toggle switch off.

Silva shook his head in disbelief. "Have I mentioned that Richardson is a real ass?"

"Not in the last twenty minutes," Jonesy replied, smirking.

"Thanks. Now why don't you see if you can keep us in the area, without doing any wild Himalayan turns, while Morris and I do some quick planning."

"I can do that," Jonesy replied with a smile.

Silva returned his smile as he left the cockpit. Morris followed.

Silva grabbed the map he'd brought and spread it out on the cabin floor and then motioned for the other men to come closer. He pulled a grease pencil out of his shirt pocket and circled an area on the map. "OK, here's the river and the substation, and this is about where the balloon is hung up on the line. The ground is scorched under the balloon, so we don't need to worry any more about the balloon exploding from a fire, and fortunately the wind is actually pushing the fire northeast away from the balloon. The area southwest has wash gullies, but otherwise is pretty flat. That's going to be our drop zone…just southwest of the target," he said making an x on the map.

Morris looked at Silva and hesitantly asked, "Are we dropping the A-5 with the firefighting equipment?"

"Absolutely. We never trust wind or fire, right?" Silva asked, looking at the circle of men, who nodded in agreement. "OK, A-5s first pass. Then you'll jump in teams of eight and nine." Silva points to the men. "Team One…Morris, Boyle, Sawyer, Davis, Williams, Clifford, Beal, and Tillis." The men acknowledged their names, and Silva continued. "Make sure the fire under the balloon is completely out, find out what's causing the line to short, and at the same time, see if you can locate the bomb or bombs, and figure out how the whole Fu-Go is hung up on the line. Work it together, and get it done fast, and then radio me as soon as you make your assessment. And let me know if you think you're going to need any special equipment that isn't in an A-5."

Silva pointed to the jump seat where Tucker sat wearing a glum face. "You're leader of Team Two."

He turned away before Tucker could protest, and began talking to Jimbo. "How many harnesses did you make?"

"I could only find enough parts for two, sir, but," he proudly held up one of the revised rigs with an extra web belt attached, "now we can also use them to climb the poles to get to the line, if we need to." Jimbo smiled and added, "And one of them is big enough for me."

"That's terrific!" Silva patted Jimbo on the back then looked around and pointed, "Roger, you're the defuser. Get Jimbo to size the second harnesses for you."

Roger stood up and playfully slapped Dixie's head. "Defuser, again…me. Dixie, I swear you must have a horseshoe up your ass. Man, you ain't never the defuser. I need to find me a good luck charm."

Dixie laughed and slapped Roger's back. "The Lord looks out for those that make music."

Roger mumbled under his breath and headed toward Jimbo.

Silva looked at Tucker. "Captain, once you get Team Two on the ground, I want you on the radio talking to me at all times. Let me know what's going on, and I'll pass the information on to the major." Silva stood up. "OK, men," his voice boomed. "The clock's ticking. Let's get moving." He looked directly at Tucker and added, "We have our orders."

The men began grouping in teams and sitting in the order they would jump. Boyle looked around, got up, and then moved to the open jump seat next to Tucker.

"Sir, I never thanked you for saving my ass after… that night," Boyle said quietly with his head down. "The Colonel would have booted me out of the army if it hadn't been for you."

"I never wanted to lose any of my men…ever…for any reason," Tucker replied back softly.

"And I want you to know…" Boyle hesitated and then sighed, "…that it was my fault Willie jumped, not yours."

Tucker cocked his head questioningly to Boyle. "Why would you think that, Sarge?"

"I wanted," Boyle started, "no, I needed to get that gondola for us...all of us, but especially you. You saved my butt with Richardson during that inspection—even after the way I'd been disrespecting you." Boyle shook his head. "I wanted to get that gondola so Richardson would get off your back. You never deserved to be treated like that by him, or by me. And Willie promised to help me. That's why he jumped...he promised to help me."

Tucker and Boyle looked at each other as tears welled in both men's eyes.

"Sergeant," Silva yelled from the open jump door, "let's drop the A-5s next pass."

Boyle stood to leave, but Tucker stopped him. "Thank you for telling me, Sergeant," he said softly. He extended his hand.

Boyle nodded and shook Tucker's hand.

"My god, Sergeant, did I just get the last word?"

Boyle smiled and then turned to the other men and shouted in his usual gruff voice. "Team One, let's get the A-5s moved to the door."

CHAPTER TWENTY-EIGHT

The Hanford power lines traversed and crisscrossed vast, desolate expanses of brown dirt, dried grasses, and thick patches of scrub brush. Even though the areas under the lines were kept mowed, the hot July sun had parched the grass until it had dried and curled up—the perfect fuel to feed a fire.

The wind picked up as the first parachutists landed, and it pushed them west of the designated drop zone. Silva had warned the men that the wind was gusting, but today's jump wouldn't be cancelled—they would just have to work with it. There wasn't another choice.

Morris worked quickly to free his chute from the brush, roll it up, and secure it. When he finished he looked around and saw three other men on the ground fighting the wind to get control of their chutes. He looked skyward to the C-47 as two more white parachutes opened against the clear, blue sky and drifted apart in different directions.

He grabbed the radio from his pack. "Bravo, this is Morris. The wind is shifting down here and I've got men all over the place," he said as he watched another parachute open.

"Team One, this is Bravo, your last jumper is in the door."

Morris looked up and watched the man jump. His chute opened and he gently floated down, until a gust of wind caught his parachute, and spilled the air out before he landed. The parachute was horizontal, and the man beside it was freefalling.

"Holy shit," Morris screamed into the radio. "The last parachute went horizontal."

"Oh, my god," Silva voice came back through the radio.

There was nothing anyone could do but watch as the paratrooper slammed into the ground.

Morris dropped the radio and ran through the dense scrub brush to help. The other jumpers on the ground followed.

"Quick." Morris pointed to the men that were with him. "Gather up the 'chute, and cut the shrouds if you need to, and for god sake don't move him."

The men got their knives out to cut the lines and remove the billowing parachute that was covering the injured jumper.

"It's Sarge," a voice yelled. "He's alive, but he's unconscious."

Morris ran closer and looked down at Boyle. He began to take off his jumpsuit. "Hang on, Sarge. We're gonna get you out of here and get you some help," he said as he transferred everything from the jumpsuit to his uniform pockets. When he was done, he handed his suit to one of the men. "Make a litter. Follow the procedure we learned in training and treat him like he has a broken back. We don't want to do more damage then has already been done."

Morris stepped back to give the men room and to put his web belt and pack back on. "Let's take him to the clearing where we stacked the A-5s. Carry him slow and easy. And keep your eyes open for the rest of the men."

The two men carefully moved Boyle onto the flattened out jumpsuit lying next to him, and with one man in the front holding the jumpsuit's legs and another man in the back holding the jumpsuit's arms, they lifted Boyle and headed for the clearing.

The three missing men appeared out of a thicket of brush. Two of the men were holding up Sawyer, who was hopping on one leg.

"Twisted my ankle when I landed," Sawyer told Morris as the men helped him sit down with his back against one of the A-5s.

"Looks like we're two men short now," Morris said.

Sawyer saw Boyle around the corner of the stacked A-5s. "What happened? Is he OK?"

"Sarge went horizontal and got slammed. He had a hard fall and is out cold. I just hope he didn't break his back." Morris shook his head, looking at Boyle. "But I don't know."

"Sawyer, you stay right here and keep an eye on the sergeant. Do you have the first-aid kit and morphine with you?"

"Yes, sir. Right here." Sawyer patted his backpack.

"OK," he said, squeezing Sawyer's shoulder before he turned to the other men gathered around them.

"The rest of you men—with me. Let's see if we can get that balloon."

CHAPTER TWENTY-NINE

From the door of the circling C-47, Silva watched smoke rippled back and forth across the scorched ground. As he scanned the area, he saw grass and brushes on the northern side of the power lines suddenly burst into flames.

The fire, fanned by the gusting and changing wind, had turned westward.

"No," Silva yelled. He hit the side of the jump door open handed and then picked up the radio. "Team One. Can you hear me? Morris...please! If you can hear me, the wind's done a one-eighty. The fire turned and is moving fast toward you."

Tucker heard him and rushed to the door.

"I need to talk to Jonesy," Silva said, handing the radio to Tucker as he stood up and headed for the cockpit.

Morris's voice boomed over the radio. "Bravo. We've got a problem. Boyle's unconscious. His back may be broken. And Sawyer can't walk. The other men and I were just heading to the balloon, but a fire is spreading between our position and the balloon."

Tucker looked below and saw the fire was raging uncontrolled through an area of dried brush northwest of the men on the ground.

"Morris, stay were you are," Tucker said excitedly into the radio, "and get the A-5 with the firefighting equipment unpacked. Now!"

"OK, I'll get the men working on it. But remember I'm down two—Sawyer and the sergeant—and Boyle is really bad. He needs help."

Silva joined Tucker in the door of the C-47 again. "Tell him the men need to clear a firebreak to the northeast. Hopefully, that'll hold the fire back and give them time for two men to carry Boyle southwest to the river. I'll get Wesley to arrange a pickup there."

Morris's voice cut in. "Heard him. Sawyer did something to his ankle and he can hardly walk. If I send Sawyer, and Boyle with two men carrying him, to the river, that'll still leave four of us here, but I'm not sure we can make it through the fire to get to the balloon."

"No. I'm not sure you can either, Lieutenant." Tucker looked at Silva. "We'll work something out. Meantime, you work on the firebreak to protect yourselves. And keep your radio on."

"Will do, sir."

Silva looked at Tucker. "I guess I'd better let the Major know what's going on." Tucker nodded and followed him to the cockpit.

CHAPTER THIRTY

Richardson paced back and forth across the floor inside the control tower. "What the hell are they doing?" He looked at his watch and then up at the wall clock.

Major Wesley and Terrance sat silently at the console. They knew it was a rhetorical question, so they continued to stare quietly out of the window overlooking the runway.

Silva's voice suddenly interrupted the silence. "Tower One, this is Bravo, come in."

Wesley reached for the microphone, and Richardson and Nick moved up behind him.

"Silva, what's going on?" Wesley asked, forgetting radio protocol. "Have they gotten the balloon off the line yet?"

"No," Silva's voice answered. "We have a problem. The fire intensified and it turned. It's between Team One and the balloon. Morris has two injured men, one seriously, who we need to evac…."

Richardson grabbed the microphone from Wesley. "Put Captain Freeman on the line," he yelled. "Now!"

Silva toggled the radio switch to speaker and then handed the headset to Tucker.

"Yes, sir?"

"Freeman, your priority is to get that goddamn balloon off that wire. There will be no evacuation. No firefighting. Nothing else."

"Sir, I'll get the balloon, but I need to help the men that are getting trapped by the fire too. I have a plan…."

"Are you goddamn deaf, Freeman? I don't give a shit about another plan. Your only job is to get that goddamn balloon off the wire…period. And I don't give a damn about…"

Richardson's line filled with static.

"Sorry, sir I couldn't…." Tucker's voice in the tower was replaced with static.

The connection was gone.

Richardson threw the microphone on the console. "Goddamn it. One simple goddamn job, and he wants to talk about evacuating people." He turned to the door. "Lieutenant, I need to call headquarters, and the operation field office."

Lieutenant Davis jumped up from the console and followed Richardson out the tower control room door.

As soon as the door shut Wesley and Terrance looked at each other. "You don't think…?" Terrance asked, leaving the sentence dangling.

"Yeah, I do think—Jonesy." Wesley smiled "See if you can get Tucker or Silva back on the line."

CHAPTER THIRTY-ONE

Tucker patted Jonesy on the back. "Thank you!"

"He was wasting our time," Jonesy said as he looked at his watch. "And we don't have it to waste."

Silva stood up from the copilot seat. "You're right about that." He looked at Tucker. "You said you had a plan—let's hear it."

Dixie appeared at the door next to Tucker.

"We heard. What do we need to do to help them?"

"Get the map and lay it out. Then gather the men," Tucker said. Dixie nodded and left. Tucker turned to Jonesy. "Can you give me two more passes? We should be ready then."

"You got it."

Tucker and Silva walked back to the cabin, where Dixie had the map spread out. Tucker kneeled down by the map and the others leaned in.

"Since we only have two harnesses to get out on the line," Tucker began, "we shouldn't need more than four men...Jimbo, Roger, Dixie, and me...to get to the balloon."

Tucker looked at Jimbo and Roger and continued, "You two will climb and assess, then defuse." He looked at Silva. "Dixie and I will coordinate with you and stand by to do whatever else is needed to help Jimbo and Roger."

Silva nodded but didn't interrupt as Tucker continued. "That frees Jackson, and the other men to jump here." He pointed to a place on the map southwest of Morris and his men. "They'll be well clear of the fire area, and close enough to Team One to get to them fairly quickly."

"I agree that Morris needs more help," Silva said, "but I'm not sure we should spare five men."

Jonesy yelled from the cockpit, "Morris needs to talk to someone!"

Silva picked up the cabin headset as he looked out the jump door and saw the fire and smoke quickly nearing the area where Team One had landed.

CHAPTER THIRTY-TWO

The line of brush fires was blazing northwest of Team One, and a thin layer of smoke blanketed the air over them.

Two men used their Pulaski tools to clear brush and grass to make a long, three-foot-wide firebreak just a hundred yards from where the wounded men were resting.

Sawyer wrapped his sprained ankle with an elastic bandage and was hobbling around the unopened A-5s taking care of Boyle, who was still unconscious, when another man was brought in screaming. The man's khaki pants had caught on fire just above his jump boots, and the skin up to his knees was burnt and bleeding. Sawyer grabbed a Morphine syrette from his first-aid kit and lifted the man's shirt to give him a shot.

"Doctor Silva," Morris said into the radio, "Williams got caught in a flash fire. His legs are burned pretty badly and he can't walk. The fire's getting closer and there's no way I can carry two men on litters and help Sawyer hobble outta here."

"Morris, help is on the way. We're dropping five men to you. When they get there, you need to be ready to leave and move the wounded men to the river. Just keep moving southwest."

"But that'll only leave four men to get the balloon off the line."

"Yeah, I know it's crazy, but the captain's come up with a good plan. Four is all he's going to need, and actually I don't know if more men would even be useful."

"Sir, I know what our mission is, so if you can't…"

Tucker's voice came over the speaker and interrupted Morris. "Morris, we'll take care of the balloon, but we're not going to lose any men doing it. I'll see you back at the base. Over and out."

Morris turned and looked at the wounded men next to the A-5s, and then to the men who were desperately working on the firebreak, and then to the C-47 circling overhead in the clear, blue sky. Tears welled in his eyes.

CHAPTER THIRTY-THREE

Tucker put the headset back on the hook by the door, looked at his watch and turned to Silva.

"My watch says we've got forty-eight minutes."

"Mine too," Silva said as he looked at his watch. "I'm going to drop the wind streamers this pass. Then you and your men jump next pass."

Tucker nodded and walked to the seated men. He stopped in front of Jackson. "Tell Jonesy that Silva's dropping the streamer, then it'll be four jumpers next pass." Jackson did a mock salute and headed to the cockpit.

Tucker looked at Jimbo. "Got your tools?"

Jimbo patted the pack on his chest under his secondary chute. "They's right here."

"And the harnesses?"

Roger piped up. "I have one, and Dixie's got the one for Jimbo."

Dixie patted the pack on his chest. "And I've got the radio."

"OK," Tucker said as he turned to Silva. "Looks like we're ready.

Silva paused and looked at the four jumpers. "Stand up and hook."

The men hooked their static lines to the rod.

Silva laid down at the left side of the open door and looked at the streamers that had settled on the ground after the last pass. When the plane entered the drop zone, he patted Jimbo's left leg. Jimbo jumped. At Silva's command, Roger and Dixie followed Jimbo. When Tucker stepped up to the door, Silva looked up and quietly said, "Good luck, Captain." Then he tapped Tucker's left leg. Tucker jumped.

Silva stood up and watched the four chutes float effortlessly to the ground. The wind remained calm. He turned to the five remaining men. "We're approaching the second jump site. Remember to get as close to Team One as you can, but stay southwest."

The men nodded.

"OK men, stand up and hook."

Silva took his place at the door and didn't stand up again until all five men were off the plane, sailing downward under open parachutes, in a calm wind.

"Bring them all back," he whispered under his breath.

CHAPTER THIRTY-FOUR

The H-frame utility pole configuration that brought high-voltage power to Hanford was made when two creosote-treated Douglas fir poles set sixty feet high and fourteen feet apart where connected near the top by an eighteen-foot, horizontal wooden brace that extended two feet beyond each pole. An x brace, introduced by Hughes Brothers in the 1920s, was placed under the horizontal brace for the added stability that was needed to carry five wires three hundred feet to the next pole.

Tucker, Jimbo, Roger, and Dixie landed less than two hundred yards from the H-frame closest to the balloon. As soon as their feet hit the ground, they removed their harnesses, quickly rolled up their parachutes, and then ran across the scorched grass to get a closer look at the deflated balloon that was twenty-five feet from the H-frame.

The seventy-foot balloon was draped over the top two high-tension wires and fell beneath like a sheet hanging out to dry on a clothesline. A couple of its shrouds and tether lines were flapping in the breeze, wrapping and unwrapping themselves around the exposed lines next to the balloon.

The men walked under the power lines and stared up at the huge fluttering, paper balloon and shrouds, but couldn't see the gondola or bombs, or what caused the line to short.

"Any idea what's causing the short?" Tucker finally asked the others. "I can't see anything—can any of you?"

"No, sir," Jimbo answered, still staring up. "But I bet that metal ring's somewhere under that mess causing the trouble."

"I agree." Tucker nodded, then pointed to the H pole. "Roger, I need you and Jimbo to each climb one of the H poles."

Roger looked at Jimbo and nodded. "As long as those contraptions he made will work, we can do it."

"Great." Tucker grinned. "That'll put each of you on one of the two lines that the Fu-Go's hung up on. Work your way out on your line and see if you can lift an edge of the balloon to see what's going on underneath, and then let me know. But be really careful moving the balloon since we can't see how many bombs there are or where they are."

Both men nodded.

Tucker turned to Dixie. "Get Silva on the radio and then keep it open."

"Will do, sir."

Roger and Jimbo tightened the new harnesses over their uniforms, and Roger signaled Tucker. "Ready."

"Wait," Jimbo called to Roger. "Hook a let-down line to your harness, just in case we need it."

"I don't need to drag more weight up that pole."

Jimbo crossed his arms and arched his eyebrow at Roger.

"OK, OK." Roger picked up the coiled line and attached it the back of his web belt. Then he said to Tucker, "OK. Now we're ready to climb."

"We're getting ahold of Silva to make sure the power is still off, so don't go further than the cross bar until I give you the OK."

"Yes, sir," Roger said as he and Jimbo began to climb the two parallel poles using their knees and the new harness that was wrapped around the pole to scoot upward.

"Hey, Jimbo!" Roger yelled in the direction of the other pole. "This thing really does work."

"You didn't need to be no seer to know that!" Jimbo yelled back.

On the ground, Dixie handed the radio to Tucker. "Got Doctor Silva."

"Captain, is everything OK?" Silva's voice asked concerned.

"Yes, sir. Roger and Jimbo are climbing now. The balloon is out about twenty-five feet from the H-frame, and I wanted to make certain the power is still off before they go out on the wire."

"Yup, I just talked to Wesley. It's still off."

Tucker gave Roger a thumbs up, as Silva continued. "But everyone at Pendleton and the Hanford substation is panicky. We've got just over thirty minutes. Can you do it?"

"I'll let you know in about five minutes. The balloon is draped across the upper set of wires and hanging down over the lower set of wires, so we can't see what the problem is yet."

"Let me know as soon as you find what's causing the short."

"Did the other men get to Morris's team?" Tucker asked.

"Yeah. Jackson and the other four men landed. They're making a firebreak to cover their backs so they can carry the wounded men out."

"Good news."

"And Richardson found out what we've done and is yelling, but that's nothing new. You just worry about that balloon. The major's sending an evacuation team to meet Team One at the river and said that he'll take care of Richardson."

"Roger and Jimbo just got to the top of their poles, I'll get back to you in a minute." Tucker handed the phone back to Dixie without waiting for Silva's reply.

Sixty feet up, Roger and Jimbo reached the top of their parallel poles and worked their way across the horizontal board to the line connections.

"Twenty-five feet sure looks farther when you're up in the air than it does on the ground," Roger said.

"Come on, Rog," Jimbo coaxed, "we're gonna run outta time."

"Jimbo, are you sure this strap is goin' to hold me on a wire?" Roger yelled across the space that separated him from Jimbo.

"I got a good feeling about this, Rog." Jimbo called back.

"I don't give a shit about your feelings. I want to know if this contraption is going to hold my ass!"

"Tell you what...I'll go first...If the strap holds *my* fat ass, you know you're good!" Jimbo threw the loose end of the four-foot strap attached to his harness over the power line and reconnected it to the other end in the front of his harness. He grabbed the line and pushed off the pole.

He let go and the strap on the harness held. He was suspended below the line.

Jimbo began pulling himself, hand over hand, toward the balloon. “You coming, Rog?”

Roger threw his strap over the electric line, attached it to his harness as Jimbo had shown him, and hand over hand, he followed Jimbo toward the balloon on his parallel line.

“You doing OK?” Tucker shouted up from the ground.

“Yeah,” Jimbo answered from the edge of the balloon. “But these balloon lines sure are a tangled mess.”

“Twenty-three minutes,” Tucker called. “Can you see the ring or the bombs?”

“Not yet, but they’re under here somewhere. We’ll find them.”

Roger finally made it to his side of the balloon. “Whew-y!” He called over to Jimbo, who was working on the tangled shrouds on his line. “I sure weren’t meant to be no lineman.”

Roger cut enough shrouds on his line to be able to stick his head under the draped balloon. He pulled his head and yell, “Oh, shit!” Then he put his head under the balloon for second look.

Jimbo stopped cutting the shrouds on his line. "What you got, Rog?"

Roger poked his head out from under the balloon, again. "The ring ain't on these two lines. It's caught on the two lines below us."

Jimbo tried to move the shrouds and balloon on his line out of his way so he could have a look, but they were too tangled. "Darn, I can't see nothin' under this mess."

"Well take my word for it. We got to go down and out on the two left wires below us." Roger stuck his head under the balloon again and took another look. "And it looks like the ring might've fused itself to both of the wires."

"That'd sure make the power line short."

"What's going on?" Tucker called up.

"We got to go down the pole," Roger yelled back down. "The ring's on the middle and left wires of the three wires below us."

"Is there a bomb attached?"

"I can't tell yet. The balloon and shrouds are hanging all over the ring and gondola."

Tucker looked at his watched and called back up. "Seventeen minutes...get moving!"

Dixie looked at Tucker, and without saying anything, handed him the radio.

Tucker smiled and took it.

"Bravo, this is Team Two. Come in."

"Did you find the problem?" Silva asked excitedly.

"Yeah, it's what the major thought—the ring. It's fused two of the three power line wires carried by the horizontal brace."

"Is there a bomb?"

"They don't know yet."

"Are they taking the ring off the wires now?"

"Not yet," Tucker said hesitantly. "The ring is fused to the two wires below them. They need to go down the pole and out again."

"Damn! We're running out of time."

"Yeah. They're on the pole now," Tucker said, looking up at the two men readjusting their harnesses to go down the pole to the lower set of power lines. "They should be out to it in a few minutes."

"We've only got a little more than ten minutes," Silva said. "Let me know as soon as they get the ring off the line, and if there's a bomb."

"Will do."

Tucker handed the radio back to Dixie. They both looked up and watched as Roger and Jimbo pulled themselves out onto the two lower power line wires and disappeared under the draped balloon.

A minute later, Roger reappeared and called down at Tucker and Dixie. "The ring's melted to both lines. And there's a single bomb hanging under it, but I can't reach it. Jimbo's trying to make something I can use to move it closer to me."

Tucker shook his head. "Seven minutes, Roger!"

"I'm working as fast as I can," Roger said with beads of sweat dabbling his forehead. He lifted the balloon, pulled himself under it, and disappeared again.

Tucker turned to Dixie. "Call Silva and let him know what's going on."

Twenty seconds later, Roger reappeared from under the balloon. "We can't get it closer to either one of us.

I'm gonna hook my harness to my let-down and try to lower myself to the bomb."

"That's too dangerous!" Tucker shouted.

"Yeah, but we're out of choices." Roger unhooked the let-down rope. "Besides Jimbo the Seer told me we were gonna get this done." He held onto the loose end of the rope and heaved the coiled end over the power line.

His quick movement made the line he was on begin to sway.

Jimbo popped up from under the balloon on the other line holding a handful of tools. "What the heck are you doing, Rog..."

Jimbo's quick movement made his line begin to bounce. "Oh, shit."

A high-pitched grinding, scraping metallic sound reverberated under the balloon.

Roger and Jimbo glanced at each other and froze as their line shook in opposition.

The twisting metal screeched louder, and then popped.

Tucker and Dixie looked up just as the ring broke free from both lines and appeared with its attached bomb below the balloon.

They both gasped loudly as they watched the bomb fall in slow motion toward the ground. A second later the intact gondola exposed itself with its shrouds still attached to the limp white, seventy-foot balloon draped across the power lines. The balloon leisurely began to undrape itself and, inch by inch, slowly slither through the wires following the gondola and bomb to the ground.

Roger lurched and grabbed a handful of the balloon as it slowly slipped by. Then he grabbed another handful trying desperately to reel the sliding balloon back up.

When Jimbo saw what Roger was doing, he dropped the tools in his hand, and quickly grabbed a handful of shrouds as they slid downward in front of him.

From the ground, Tucker and Dixie watched with open mouths as the bomb, ring, and balloon continued their slow descent to the ground.

"My god," Tucker whispered.

On their separate power lines, Roger and Jimbo continued to grab handfuls of balloon and shrouds, frantically fighting to pull them back up.

The tension on the shroud lines finally became taunt.

They'd stopped the balloon's decent.

But the bomb was seven feet above the ground—nose down.

Dazed, Dixie dropped the radio. "Sweet Jesus."

"Can you hold it?" Tucker called, terrified.

"Not for long." Roger yelled as beads of sweat rolled off his forehead and dripped into his eyes.

"Dixie!" Jimbo shouted. "I dropped my wire cutters and screwdriver. They're down there somewhere."

Dixie and Tucker ran under the power line and frantically walked around searching.

Tucker looked up to make sure they were under Jimbo's position on the line and then got on his hands and knees, sweeping the burnt grass with his hands.

He found them.

"Thank god for burnt grass." He held the cutters and screwdriver out to Dixie.

Dixie took them and let out a big sigh. He stepped under the hanging bomb—a thirty-three-pound antipersonnel bomb. His mind began going over everything he'd learned about them in class as he carefully unscrewed the bomb's cast steel nose and exposed three wires, red, blue, and yellow. He touched all three.

"The blue one, Dixie!" Roger shouted. "Cut the goddamn blue one first."

"I knew that," Dixie said to himself and cut the blue wire. He was ready to call "Clear!" when he heard Wesley's voice in his mind, telling the men not to ever let an antipersonnel bomb drop on its nose, even if you think it's defused—just in case.

He drew a deep breath and felt around above the bomb's tail fins.

"Hurry up, Dixie!" Roger yelled from above. "I'm losing my grip."

"Captain, I need your help!" Dixie yelled.

Tucker rushed to his side.

"I need you to lift the bomb a little to take the tension off so I can cut the yoke. Then we need to lay it on the ground."

Without a word, Tucker gently bear hugged the bomb and lifted it slightly.

"Good." Dixie cut the yoke, threw the tools down, and grabbed for the bomb to help Tucker lower it to the ground away from the hovering gondola.

Tucker looked up and shouted to Roger and Jimbo, "Clear! Drop the balloon, and get off the lines! We've only got two minutes left."

Roger and Jimbo immediately let go of the balloon and shrouds and began moving hand over hand back to the safety of the wooden poles.

The gondola hit the ground with a loud thud and was followed by a gently wavering paper balloon.

Tucker picked the radio up off the ground. "Silva, the bomb's defused and the ring's off the line," he reported, relieved. "Roger and Jimbo are moving to the poles. Give us ten more seconds to get them off the line."

"Captain, this is Major Wesley, you're patched through to us also. Congratulations."

All of the men could hear Richardson's voice in the background.

"Oh shit!" Wesley's voice shouted over the radio. "Richardson's already made the call to Hanford to turn the power on. Tell them to get off the wire—now!"

Tucker looked up. Roger and Jimbo were still five feet from the pole. He dropped the radio, cupped his hands, and screamed. "The wire's going hot!" Tucker blew out a breath, hard. "I'd like to kill that goddamn man."

Dixie walked up next to him. "I'll help, sir."

Jimbo and Roger pitched their bodies forward and grabbed the wooden poles just as they heard the humming sound of the power course through the lines.

"Holy shit, Jimbo, I swear I could feel the electricity coming behind me. Did my hair turn gray?" Roger asked hanging onto the H-frame's wooden crossbar.

Jimbo sighed and shook his head. "That was a little too close, Rog. But your hair ain't gray."

"Well you couldn't have convinced me of that thirty seconds ago."

Both men began descending the wooden poles, as Tucker and Dixie watched.

“If Roger doesn’t fall from that pole,” Dixie said, “I’m gonna kill him when he gets down here. He put a jinx on me so I’d have to be the defuser.”

Tucker looked amused, and relieved. “How about helping me wrap up Richardson’s balloon and bomb.” Tucker smiled broadly. “And when we get back, the suds are on me at Betty’s.”

“Did I hear that you’re buying?” Roger asked as he stood on the ground unhooking the harness Jimbo had made.

“Whatever you want!”

“Didn’t I tell you I had a good feelin’ about this?” Jimbo asked as he looked at Roger.

“What I do know is that I ain’t never seen your black ass move that fast,” Roger said as he handed Jimbo his harness. “I got to admit this thing really worked.”

“Why don’t you hang on to it, Rog? I might just get myself a patent and make a lot of money. Then you’d have the original model. Should be some money in that for you too.”

Roger playfully smacked his arm as Jimbo turned to Dixie and asked, "And what'd you do with my wire cutter and screwdriver?"

Dixie pointed to the ground under the balloon.

"You threw my cutters on the ground? No one in this outfit seems to care about another man's stuff. Dixie, if I treated your sax like that..."

Tucker interrupted with a smile. "Come on men, let's pack up and get out of here."

He turned to Dixie. "Call Wesley, and ask him to send a truck for a complete Fu-Go—and us!"

CHAPTER THIRTY-FIVE

Tucker, Morris, and Wesley stood at attention in front of Richardson's large wooden desk. Silva stood next to them.

Red faced, Richardson paced the floor behind his desk, while Lieutenant Davis stood next to the desk taking notes. He'd filled several pages since Richardson began his tirade twenty minutes earlier.

Richardson stopped pacing, flattened his hands, locked his elbows, leaned on the desk, and looked at the four men in front of him. "I am sick and tired of each of you disobeying my orders."

Wesley spoke up. "Colonel, we..."

"Shut up. I'll deal with you in a minute."

Richardson looked at Silva. “First, I want you off my base immediately. You get out of my office and go pack…”

Hazel opened the office door and stepped in. “Colonel,” she began.

Richardson face turned redder when he saw her. “Goddamn it, Hazel, get out of here. I’m sick and tired of you too.”

A uniformed man with a chest full of military ribbons pushed past Hazel.

“Colonel,” the man said, “I’m General George Garrett. We’ve spoken on the phone, several times.”

Richardson and Nick came to attention.

Hazel smirked at Richardson and then left, closing the door behind her.

“General, I was just…” Richardson started.

The general ignored him, and looked at the men standing in front of the desk. “At ease, gentlemen.” The general walked in front of them and stopped by Silva. He extended his hand. “You must be Doctor William Silva.”

"Yes, sir, I am. But please call me Bill, or Silva," he said as he shook the general's hand. "I'm pleased to meet you."

"Well, young man, I sure have heard a lot about you." He winked at Silva. "And from a very reliable source."

Silva blushed.

The general smiled and turned to Wesley, Tucker, and Morris. "How fortunate to find everyone I wanted to talk to…together…in one place…imagine."

"Sir, I was just telling…" Richardson started again.

General Garrett interrupted him with a dismissive wave of his hand. "Colonel, please." He turned back to the others. "Gentlemen, the president asked me to come here and personally congratulate the 555th Airborne Infantry, Major Wesley, Doctor Silva, and," he looked harshly at Richardson, "the Colonel, for what you all did at Hanford."

He moved closer to Tucker and put his hand on Tucker's shoulder. "Captain Freeman, what you and your men accomplished there, without losing a man, was… well nothing short of extraordinary. And in the next few weeks after the whole story comes out, I think you'll be able to fully understand and appreciate the importance of what you did yesterday, and how catastrophic it would have been if you failed."

General Garrett turned around to Richardson. "And Colonel, I'm especially happy to inform you that your leadership of these fine men has also been noticed. Effective today you're reassigned to headquarters. You'll be working for me until you retire…as soon as the war ends."

Richardson stood open mouthed.

"Have your aide help you gather your belongings. I'll be back in an hour to take you back to Walla Walla with me."

Garrett turned back to the others. "And speaking of Walla Walla, I went to visit Sergeant Boyle in the hospital today. A couple of broken ribs and a concussion—he'll be discharged from the hospital in a week or two. He was one lucky man. The doctor said he couldn't believe that Boyle didn't have more injuries. Apparently those football helmets you all wear really work," he said with a broad smile. "OK. Let's go to the Officers' Club, I want to hear, firsthand, the whole story about the fire and the balloon, and the bomb falling from the wires. Must have been pretty exciting."

Garrett looked back at Richardson. "Oh, and Hazel will be going to the club with us," he said as he opened the door for the others. "One hour, Colonel."

He closed the door behind him, leaving Richardson and Davis standing at attention, speechless.

As the men followed the general out of the office, Tucker leaned toward Wesley. "Major, Morris and I aren't allowed in the Officers' Club," he whispered.

Wesley chuckled and patted Tucker on the back. "You're the guest of General George Garrett. Believe me, no one will say anything to you."

CHAPTER THIRTY-SIX

The Pendleton Field Officers' Club lounge had been built in 1941 to serve the hundreds of officers of the 17th Bombardment Group and the other units that supported them. It was spacious and elegantly decorated with oriental rugs and original oil paintings of uniformed men and airplanes. Overstuffed chairs and deep leather couches enclosed by end tables and cocktail tables were arranged in groupings throughout the lounge. And even though there were only a handful of officers still at the base, the club remained open for them.

Hazel and Silva sat together on a couch, while the others took chairs around the large, square, birds-eye maple cocktail table in front of the couch.

A fiftyish, short waiter with graying hair approached the gathering. He tilted his head and looked at Tucker and Morris with a painted smile. He then tugged at the front of his crisply starched white jacket and turned to General Garrett. "What can I get for you today, sir?"

"You can bring us a bottle of your best champagne," Garrett said as he looked at the waiter's name, "and six champagne glasses please, Thomas. We've got some celebrating to do."

"Of course, sir." Thomas turned, and looked at Tucker and Morris as he left.

General Garrett watched the waiter walked away. "Our way of thinking will change someday," he said reflectively, "and we'll all be the better for it."

Everyone sat in silence for a moment.

"You know, Major," Garrett said turning to Wesley, "the army needs a new CO here. I recommended you, and it's been approved."

Wesley was taken aback by the surprise announcement. He had planned on making the army his career, but thought it would be a while before he would be considered for a command post—even for a skeletal base. "Thank you, sir."

"I'm just sorry to have to tell you that the only aide available is Lieutenant Davis." Garrett laughed. "But for some reason I don't think he'll be a problem anymore."

Garrett took a piece of paper out of his breast pocket and handed it to Wesley. "And, of course, the job does come with a promotion to Lieutenant Colonel. We'll get you pinned this afternoon before I leave."

Wesley looked at the paper in shocked disbelief. Tucker, Morris, and Silva stood to shake hands with Wesley and offer their congratulations.

The waiter returned with a bottle and presented the label to the general. Garrett nodded in approval as he read: Moët & Chandon's 1936 Dom Pérignon. He looked at Thomas and smiled. "Excellent. This fits the occasion perfectly. Thank you, Thomas."

Thomas smiled and signaled for two other waiters to bring out the ice bucket and a tray with six glasses. He popped the cork and filled the six glasses, placed one on the table in front of everyone and then turned to the general. "Will you be needing anything else, sir?"

"No, not right now. But thank you, Thomas."

The general picked up his glass and stood. The others followed his lead. "To the Triple Nickles," he said, raising his glass. "The army and the nation owe you our gratitude."

"Thank you, sir," Tucker and Morris said in unison as everyone took a sip from their champagne glass.

Garrett raised his glass again. "And here's to Pendleton Field's new CO—Lieutenant Colonel Charles Wesley."

"Here, here!" Silva piped up as he nodded to Wesley.

Again everyone raised their glasses.

Wesley acknowledged his friends with a nod and a smile.

Then Garrett raised his glass a third time. "And, lastly, I want to congratulate my beautiful niece, Hazel, on her engagement to Doctor Silva. And her pending new career as a high school math teacher in Missoula."

Tucker, Morris, and Wesley looked at each other, flabbergasted.

"Thank you, Uncle George, but the engagement," Hazel said looking sternly at Silva, "isn't exactly official yet."

"Oh, yes it is. He asked permission for your hand on the way over here, and I said yes!"

Hazel set her champagne on the table and put her hands on her hips. "Excuse me. But I'm the one he needs to ask," she said flatly, looking from her uncle to Silva.

Garrett shrugged at Silva.

Hazel smiled and winked at Silva. "Well, OK. I accept." She leaned forward to hug him as he let out a big sigh.

Garrett turned to the three other men and whispered, "I tried to warn him. He's sure going to have his hands full. That girl wants to be the boss of everyone… even a general!"

Everyone chuckled, clinked their glasses, and finished their champagne.

General Garrett sat back down and took a card and a pen out of his pocket. He wrote something on the back of it and then turned to Wesley. "I better pick up the

Colonel and get back to headquarters. We've got a lot of paperwork to do this afternoon, and before I leave I want to put those silver oak leaves on you to make it official."

"Yes, sir." Wesley said as he stood and picked up his hat.

Garrett walked over to Tucker. "Captain, I appreciate and am grateful for everything you and your men did yesterday. And they deserve to celebrate too." He handed the card to Tucker. "I want your men to go to the NCO club, as my personal guests."

"Sir, I don't think..."

"You tell one of them to give the manager that card. I assure you there won't be any problems."

"Yes, sir." Tucker put the card in his shirt pocket. "Thank you."

"No, Captain, thank you." He put his hand out to Tucker and they shook.

Garrett turned to Wesley. "Ready, Colonel?"

"Indeed I am, sir."

Wesley turned to Tucker. "Debriefing 0800. Hangar A."

"Yes, sir, colonel."

He paused to look at Hazel. "And Hazel, I don't expect to see you walk in tomorrow!"

Hazel stood and gave Wesley a mock salute before she turned to her uncle. "Thank you," she whispered as she gave Garrett a long hug.

She turned to Silva with a mischievous smile then took her fiancée's hand and kissed him softly.

EPILOGUE

Pendleton Field Train Station

Two Months Later

Tucker and Morris stood by the last car on the train platform talking while the rest of the men stowed their gear and staked out a seat inside the troop sleeper.

"I guess you will have been processed out by the time I get back to Mackall," Tucker said sadly.

"Yup, Pearl's already back there waiting for me, and we'll be heading to New York the minute I get my papers. I'm sure happy this war is over."

"I am too. It's still hard to believe that Hanford was making the plutonium for the Nagasaki bomb. It really would have been catastrophic if we didn't get the power on."

"Or if the bomb you were defusing would've hit the ground."

"We made a fine team, Morris. Sure you don't want to stay in?"

"I'm sure. Pearl and I want to settle down and start a family. We need to be around people like us. The military is too hard a life for a family."

"I wish you both the best. But I'm sure going to miss having you around."

"I think it's great that you're staying in, Captain. The army needs teachers and mentors that will inspire *our* men and teach them to be proud. Your grandfather influenced your way of thinking, and now you get to pass it on." Morris smiled. "The first day I met you, you said that you wanted to be a teacher. Looks to me like you got your wish." Morris put his hand out to Tucker.

Tucker took it and then pulled him closer and gave him a hug. "Keep in touch. And if you're passing through DC in two weeks, I expect to see you at my wedding."

"We're going to try to make it. And you and Dorothy have a standing invitation to visit us in New York anytime."

The train whistle blew, and Morris moved to the door. He stopped and turned back to Tucker, giving him a crisp salute. Then he boarded the train without looking back.

As the train began to pull out of the station, the men opened the windows in their train car and waved good-bye.

He waved back with tears in his eyes.

Tucker watched the train until it was well out of the station. Then he slowly walked from the platform toward the front of the station where *Lucille* was waiting for him, a wedding present from the Triple Nickles.

A lot has certainly happened since the first time I was at this station, he thought as he walked toward the street. *Lucille is waiting for me instead of the Ebenezer Baptist Church bus, I'm not trying to figure out what the heck we're doing here, and...* His thoughts were interrupted when he saw Terrance, wearing civilian clothes, sitting on a bench under the Greyhound Bus sign.

"Terrance, what are you doing here?" Tucker asked.

"The army let the cooks and other servicemen muster out here instead of going back to Mackall, if we wanted, so I'm heading back to Philadelphia."

"I knew you were getting out, but I thought you and Betty had something going. I was sure you were going to settle here."

"Naw. She looked awful good once a week, but every day was too much."

Tucker chuckled, and Terrance continued. "And you know, when all the guys started leaving, well, this town got to looking a little too white to me."

"You have family in Philadelphia?"

"Not any more. But I imagine I can find a room somewhere with my three hundred dollars mustering out money. Then I'm gonna go back to school. I always wanted to be a teacher. Help kids get started on the right foot."

"A teacher? Really?" Tucker mused. "Isn't that something."

"Yeah. I've only got two years to go, and with that GI Bill, this sure feels like the right time."

A Greyhound bus came down the street. It stopped on the opposite side of the road waiting for a car to pass before it turned into the train station.

Terrance stood up and picked up his duffel bag. He put his hand out to Tucker. "Captain, it has been a real pleasure. I definitely learned a lot more from my time here than I ever thought I would. And most of it is thanks to you."

Tucker shook his hand. Then stopped and looked at him for a long moment.

The bus pulled in, and the door opened.

"Terrance, would you consider sitting in the front seat of a Ford convertible, instead of the backseat of a Greyhound bus to go back East?"

Terrance looked at Tucker questioningly.

"I'm driving to DC by myself, and I sure wouldn't mind having some company. The route takes me pretty close to Philadelphia anyway.

"Thanks, Captain. That sounds really good. I really appreciate the offer and I'm happy to help with gasoline and driving."

"But I do want to make one stop along the way—the army hospital in Walla Walla."

"Good. I'd like to see Sarge too."

"OK." Tucker smiled and added, "Why don't you call me *Tucker* now that you're a civilian."

Terrance nodded and followed Tucker toward *Lucille.*

"You know Terrance, my mother works at Howard University. If you don't have family or another reason to go to Philadelphia, maybe she could help you get into Howard." Tucker's mind was turning. "Hell, she takes in roomers from the university, you could stay right there."

Terrance threw his duffel bag in the backseat of the car, thinking about Tucker's offer.

Tucker opened the door on the driver's side of the car, still talking. "You two would get along real well—you're both direct, don't have time for a lot of nonsense, and aren't bashful about saying what's on your mind."

"Well, that's the truth," Terrance said furrowing his brow, still thinking.

"And I'd sure like it if she had someone to kind of be there and maybe help her out now that my fiancée is going to be moving with me as soon as we're married," Tucker continued. "Hell, you could work for your room and board."

Tucker pulled away from the station and continued talking as he and Terrance headed east, out of Pendleton, Oregon.

AUTHOR'S NOTES

The real story of the Triple Nickles and their part in "Operation Firefly" is fascinating, and my hope in writing this book is to bring recognition to a group of people who were a very important part of history, who have not be recognized enough. The following are just some of the truths that were woven into the story:

First Sergeant Walter Morris and sixteen other African-Americans graduated from the paratrooper school at Fort Benning, Georgia, in February 1944, becoming the 555th Parachute Infantry "Test Platoon." They were sent to Pendleton Field, Oregon, in May 1945 for "Operation Firefly." Of course, unlike in this novel, there were several hundred enlisted men and officers by 1945, who all became the army's first smoke jumpers.

You can read more about the Triple Nickles online at the Association's website: www.triplenickle.com.

The Triple Nickles did use their football helmets to jump, and the Forest Service adopted the practice.

The Japanese Fu-Go program sent approximately ten thousand balloon bombs across the Pacific between November 1944 and April 1945. One of them killed six Americans who were picnicking in Bly, Oregon. Today the area is called the Mitchell Recreation Area and has a monument honoring those killed. The Japanese have apologized for the deaths, and they planted several cherry trees around the monument. If you'd like more information about the Japanese Fu-Go program, I'd recommend looking at: *Smithsonian Annals of Flight (Number 9): Japan's Word War II Balloon Bomb Attacks on North America* by Robert C. Mikesh.

Japanese submarines sank two American merchant ships and damaged two others in mid-December 1941. The 17th Bombardment group sank one of the submarines on Christmas Eve 1941. The others weren't seen again.

A Triple Nickle, PFC Malvin L. Brown, was the first smoke jumper fatality when he fell out of a Douglas fir. His body was taken home to Pennsylvania in August 1946, and after a long search his gravesite was located in May 2014 near Baltimore, Maryland.

Hanford Engineering Works was a Manhattan Project site. A Fu-Go landed and shorted out one of the lines that provided the power for the nuclear cooling reactor cooling pumps. The balloon fell off the line and power was restored.

All of the side stories about Doolittle, the Great Northern Railroad, Washington DC's Union Station, Hanford Engineering Works, and Pendleton are true.

PHOTO/GRAPHIC CREDITS

Book Cover Design: Larry Behunek

Part 1: Fu-Go

Courtesy of the Smithsonian Institution Press; Number 9, *Smithsonian Annals of Flight* (1973)

Part 2: Paratroopers

Courtesy of the 555th Parachute Infantry Association, Inc.

Part 3: Smoke Jumpers

Courtesy of the 555th Parachute Infantry Association, Inc.

Part 4: Hanford

Courtesy of the Department of Energy, Hanford Site

ACKNOWLEDGEMENTS

My heartfelt thanks to: Dr. E.A. Silva for sharing the story that started me on this journey; Patricia for being a patient editor and sounding board; Larry Sutton of the Forest Service for his quick, thorough responses to all of my fire fighting questions and his encouragement to get the Triple Nickles story out; Tony Peterilli, a Missoula smoke jumper, who answered questions and graciously shared his firsthand experiences and stories; Joseph Murchison, president of the 555th Parachute Infantry Association, for putting me in touch with Walter Morris and his daughter Crystal—a life-changing experience; to the great people at CreateSpace for their editing and layout help; Kristin and Stephanie for their enthusiastic help and support;

and lastly to my husband, Tom, who encouraged me to turn my screenplay into a novel, helped with research and editing, and gave me the space and time to spend five years with Tucker Freemen and the seventeen Triple Nickles.

ABOUT THE AUTHOR

Liane Young is a retired director of corporate communications for the Office of Naval Research. She is the winner of the 2012 Virginia Screenwriting Competition for *Operation Firefly*, which tells the amazing, little-known story of the US Army's first all-black test platoon, the "Triple Nickles" 555th Parachute Infantry Battalion. She currently lives in Virginia with her husband, Tom. Between kayaking, travelling and enjoying time with her family, Young is working on her next novel, *The Himalayan Teapot.*

www.lianeyoung.com

22124199R00245

Made in the USA
Middletown, DE
20 July 2015